INSOMNIAC

A collection of bite-sized spooky stories

By Matt Gall

D1501129

"Don't Fall Asleep"

The message was broadcast into every person's head at the same time. They spent days looking for a logical explanation, eventually searching for a supernatural explanation, but came up with nothing. The top theories were that aliens sent us a message, angels came to command us to prepare for the rapture, or governments were testing some technology to mind control the population.

None of these theories had any substance, so nothing could be done. People tried to go on with their lives.

Then they started dying.

The pattern was obvious. Half the population of Earth was wiped out in one day. After people had fallen asleep, they suffered terrifying nightmares, panicking and screaming before having a heart attack.

Emergency powers were enacted, citizens practically volunteered to be sleep test subjects, feeling unsafe to crawl into their beds.

Researchers had rushed their work, and within four days they discovered that humans suffer the heart attack as soon as they start dreaming, although brain activity still functions for a few minutes after the heart stops. Animals showed no difference in their REM cycles, whatever was happening was exclusive to humans.

If you thought the "I need coffee to stay alive lol" crowd was annoying before, you should've seen the panic here. Anything caffeinated became incredibly valuable. Meth and cocaine use became a necessity, scientists had to figure out how to keep humans from dreaming, and they had to do it highly caffeinated, without sleep, possibly on stimulating drugs.

They didn't make it. Most of humanity had died off by the sixth day. Nobody can stay awake forever, and many choose suicide over a horrifying nightmare before dying.

Not even me. I'm an insomniac, I've always had trouble at night, both falling and staying asleep. It's not easy to keep awake, despite the decades of practice I've had, but I started giving myself little chores. I'd cover the bodies of the dead, scavenge as much Red Bull and Kickstart as possible, try to find scary stories so I stay up.

Twelve days awake. I'm about to beat the world record, not that there's anyone around to appreciate it. Hell, I don't know, I might be the last person left awake.

I've been hallucinating constantly since day three. I've seen the aliens come, the angels explain to me we have to be awake, government members admitting to the experiment, but I know none of it is real. I have no idea how anyone could conduct research under these mental conditions, everything feels foggy, like I'm experiencing life wading through a murky pond.

I'm lying in bed now. A bottle of sleeping pills is next to me, but I can't decide if I should swallow them, or just let me myself sleep. I have to admit I'm curious what the nightmares must be like; if they can kill off everyone on the planet, and a delirious part of me wants to experience them for myself.

I lie in bed, listen to the silence of the empty world around me, and drift into sleep.

 The Rope

The rope crashed into Earth on a Monday afternoon, catching our entire planet off guard.

The government swooped in, trying to assume control and make sense of the situation, but nobody had any answers.

The rope itself was thick, no larger than the type used for climbing exercises, but it extended up into the sky, far past how far our telescopes could see. NASA tried to locate the origin, but the rope just kept going out into space, they couldn't trace where it may have come from.

The first person to grab the rope did so as a joke. He was a guard for the landing site, deciding one day to tug on it, to "see what would happen". Immediately after his palms grasped the rope, he flew upwards, as if he was on a vertical zip line. He kept sailing up and up, finally exiting our field of vision, and later our atmosphere.

We never got in contact with him again.

The second person to grab the rope did so for an exploratory mission. He was given a backpack, a space suit, rations, and communication devices, and was told to explain as much detail as he could about his surroundings before we lost contact with him. The man knew it was a suicide mission, but couldn't resist his own curiosity.

We kept contact for five days. There was debate over how fast he was actually going, as he passed Mars within the first three hours, but the fact that he was alive, conscious, and cognitive suggested he couldn't possibly be going as fast as indicated. He described stars and the dark vastness of space, and an incredible feeling of unease.

On the fifth day, he described seeing the darkness "come towards him." His last recorded words were "the mouth is so big, it could swallow a planet!"

Whatever creature had killed him must have severed the rope, because two days after, it fell back down the Earth. The total distance of the rope he had traveled would have placed him just before Pluto, yet it had only been five days.

On the sixth day, a ship came to Earth. We aren't sure who they are, or what they are. We aren't sure if they know what the creature that destroyed the rope is, or if they think that we destroyed the rope as an act of war. We don't know if they created the rope, or just sent it to us, or if they were involved at all.

All we know is the door is opening, and we have no idea what they want.

Fear the Old Music

ONLY THOSE THAT HEAR, CAN SEE.

The green note was attached to a cassette tape, left in my mailbox. There was no return address, it wasn't even wrapped, just placed inside with the ominous quote taped on.

Naturally, I went out, bought a cheap cassette player, and listened to it.

It was strange. It sounded like odd chanting, with instruments I'd never heard before playing in the background. Voices chimed in; some would sing, some would scream, before being abruptly cut off. I felt physically ill after a few minutes of this, and rushed to turn it off.

Don't let curiosity get the best of you, I reminded myself. I didn't know who put that tape there, or why, and it was stupid of me to rush into listening to it. Just some weird creepy soundtrack by some guy that got banned from Sound cloud.

But then I started seeing THEM.

Nobody else seemed to notice them, they would just stand still in public. They looked normal, like an average, everyday person, but they didn't have heads. Glowing green triangles circles around them as they watched me go about my daily life, and even though they had no face I could tell they were grinning.

Last night I found another note in my mailbox.

FINISH THE SONG, WE REQUIRE THE FRUIT IT BEARS.

Naturally, I called the police this time. They said they'd keep an eye out, but there wasn't much else they could do. As they left, I saw a glowing triangle in the back of their squad car, watching me.

Not knowing what else to do, I listened to the rest of the tape. The same sounds played, chanting, screaming, singing, but this time my name was being whispered over and over again. I even rewound the tape and listened from the start; they definitely weren't saying my name the first time I heard it.

I didn't sleep last night, every time I heard a sound I thought it was the triangle things coming to get me. I stepped outside for a cigarette, before groaning when I noticed a thousand little green triangles in the sky, replacing all the stars. Some flicked, and I felt they were blinking at me, like a leviathan with an uncountable amount of eyes.

Naturally, I called into work the next day, and took myself to the hospital until they could find out what's wrong with me.

They ran an MRI, and found an odd growth in the front of my brain. Assuming it was a tumor I was prepped for surgery, and the growth was removed.

When I woke up, I felt relief. It was just a brain tumor causing hallucinations, there was no cult, or triangle people, or dark creature in the sky.

The doctor came to talk to me, carrying a small box. He explained that they did remove something from my head, but it wasn't a tumor.

It was a small, green triangle. It was composed of fats and proteins, both absorbed from my brain, although it was also made of random metals like beryllium and strontium.

We both sat in silence for a while, I had no explanation, and neither did the doctor. Theoretically, he said, just having that thing in my head should have killed me, yet I seemed mostly healthy upon coming in.

I snorted at that, and explained the song and triangles to him. Why not? Things were weird enough.

He nodded through my story, seeming to believe me. The doctor waited until I had finished, before admitting he heard strange sounds coming from the triangle after its removal. I gave him my apartment keys to get the tape back, to compare what was on it to what he heard.

He never came back.

The staff aren't responding. I've had my call light on for a half hour now. Bright, green light is flashing in from outside, a giant triangle floating in the sky.

I haven't seen anything about it on the news, so I don't think anyone else can see it. There's a crowd of people, well, THINGS, outside the hospital, all staring at my window with a face that isn't there.

None of them have mouths, but I can tell they're grinning.

I've barricaded the door. I can't figure out how to turn the call light off, so I have to hope the nurses keep ignoring it, if they can perceive it at all. I don't have a next step, I'm really just hoping for some kind of miracle to come.

I finished a crying session to notice a note was sliding under my door, the same green color as the other two were. I panicked and raced to see it, desperate to know if it would tell me how to end this nightmare.

YOUR FRUIT WAS MORE BEAUTIFUL THAN ANY BEFORE, WE MUST RECLAIM YOU FOR FUTURE USE. DO NOT TRY TO ESCAPE, WE WILL FIND YOU. DO NOT CALL FOR HELP, WE WILL FIND THEM. DO NOT THINK YOU CAN ESCAPE BY DYING, EVEN THROUGH HELL, WE WILL FIND YOU.

Instead of hope, I found myself slumping into my chair, not understanding any part of these events.

I switched the TV on, but the only channel that came in was video of a glowing triangle.

I looked at myself in the mirror, my face kept distorting from normal to the same green triangle I had seen on those other people.

I peeked out the hall after taking my barricade down slowly, and guess what? I saw a group of triangle people, waiting down the hall as if to greet me after surgery.

If anyone else ever gets a mysterious tape, you probably shouldn't listen to it. I'm a curious guy, I thought maybe it had been a prank or an advertisement.

Now I'm hiding in a hospital room, remarkably recovered after major brain surgery, unsure what fate has in store for me next.

Fear the old music, my friends.

Clonal groves

She wanted to go visit Pando in Utah, studying ecology. Hannah was fascinated with the concept of clonal groves; a forest connected underground by a single network of roots.

The idea of a small forest all originating from the same tree was fascinating, especially since it was almost impossible to tell. If nobody had told her what to look for, she would never have known.

Hannah snuck across the border, propped up to keep troublesome pests out; including people. Hannah excluded herself from that, she wanted some tree samples to sequence back in the lab. The sign displayed a skull and crossbones, making her snort. Most likely to keep troubled teens out from the park area.

Trees surrounded her, she felt as though something was watching her, but she spotted no other animals around her. She carved off small branches and leaves from various trees, hoping the genetic sequence would prove what she already knew; all these trees were genetically identical, stemming from the same big tree, Pando.

One tree in particular gave her a sinking feeling. The branch patterns were unique, as if they were modeled off a sculpture. She jabbed her knife in, deciding to take home some sap to sequence.

Blood burst out.

Hannah screamed, falling to the ground. Beneath the dirt, various roots emerged from the ground, pinning her. She kept screaming for help, but nobody else was around to hear her.

She felt a pinch and looked down at her arm; roots had injected themselves into her, pushing in a dark red substance similar to the blood that burst out from the tree moments before. It was….peaceful, she thought. Despite pain signals and fear rushing through her system, she felt at ease, as if she belonged here. If someone had walked by and told her this was her mark on Earth, she would have rejoiced.

Hannah felt the others in her head. The other trees around her all looked humanoid in appearance; how had she not seen that before? Their shapes became clearer as their voices became more intelligible.

stay with us

the grand tree cares for us, the world outside does not

it hurts but only for a little

She let the voices in, reaching down to scratch an itch on her leg, shuddering as she only could rake budding stems across freshly formed bark.

Hannah felt herself stand, but couldn't move. She was rooted to her spot. She felt at home, though. More at home in this world than ever before. The voices of the others connected to Pando sang along with her to the sounds of nature. The scientist in her wondered who or what Pando was, and why it connected itself to its victims, but as the wind whistled and the birds chirped, she realized it didn't matter.

She stood, rooted to the dirt, watching through eyes made of chlorophyll, waiting for the next person to join the family.

The Onsloth

Imagine how scary sloths would be if they were big and fast. They have huge claws, they move silently, and nobody would suspect them at first of causing trouble.

That was the reality of August 2021.

We all ripped on 2020 for being a bad year, but then the "Onsloth" began. Giant waves of sloths crawled out of the forests on the western side of the United States, followed by legions of normal sized, but extremely agile and bloodthirsty, sloths.

We lost the entire western seaboard within three days. Resistance was scattered across the states, as many towns and cities became prime targets for the Onsloth. Sloths are herbivores, eating a small diet of leaves, and these proved no different.

They killed just for the sake of killing, licking the blood off their claws after tearing a person apart.

We named the bigger sloths the Megatherium. We aren't sure where they came from, we think they've just been hiding from us. They have significant intelligence, knowing how and when to cut power lines during attacks. The common belief now is that every sloth had been hiding their speed and strength for generations, waiting for the Megatherium to help them change the dominant species on Earth.

My wife was slashed to pieces weeks ago. I spent nights sobbing quietly, afraid to attack the soulless grins of the sloths. I've found a small group of survivors, but we've been dwindling. I haven't seen a child in months, even the normal sized sloths we're used to can take down a grown man on their own.

We sat around a smokeless campfire, made using dried animal droppings, a group of strangers in a powerless world, all holding onto each other just to have something to hold. A faint scratching sound cut through the silence, and some of us stood up, aiming our guns staring at the direction it came in.

A tree collapsed where one woman had been sitting. She was smashed into the dirt, twitching pathetically under the bark. A giant, grinning Megatherium crawled toward us, moving slow as if to taunt us. More rustling followed, and a small legion of sloths crawled toward us, strange soulless grins on their faces.

We tried to run. In the end, we scattered. I hid under a small bush, praying to any God that was out there to let me live through the night. I listened to the agonized and drawn out shrieks as the sloths tore through my band of survivors like they were made of paper, their claws able to sever an adult in half in one swing.

I laid quietly. The fighting had died down, I was the only one left. I slowly peered out from under the bush, hoping to see nothing in the darkness.

Thousands of emotionless eyes peered at me in the darkness, claws reflecting the light of the fire.

I collapsed to my knees, hoping it would be quick.

A Just Reward

Is it better to be born virtuous, or overcome temptation by sheer force of will?

I think the latter. I had strange urges growing up. Of what I wanted to do to women, teachers, classmates. Unspeakable things. WRONG things. Things that make parents tell their kids to stay near them in public.

I was always self-aware, knew that I was different. I tried to resist the parts of me that felt WRONG, partially because I knew it was WRONG, and partially because I was afraid I would be caught. I wanted nothing more than to give into my urges; I always knew that was WRONG, so I never succumbed to temptation.

Sally was my next door neighbor, and childhood best friend. We had walked, and later driven, to school together since we were five.

Every day, for over a decade, I resisted those urges, and fought back. I never let the WRONGNESS take over. I could push Sally down this upcoming hill, or miss our next turn and drive to a secluded location, or sneak in her house before her parents got home.

Oh, I wanted to, so badly.

But that was WRONG, so I never succumbed to temptation.

Besides, I'd be the last person seen with her. They'd catch me for sure. I was a lot of bad things on the inside, but I wasn't stupid.

Even after Sally and I drifted apart, I still thought of her. Oh, there were other women I wanted to be WRONG with, but one always remembers their first, right? The women at college and work just never compared, maybe it was the connection we had as kids that always drew me back to Sally. I felt disappointed when I heard she was arrested for assault and battery at 32. She must have had some WRONGNESS just like me, but was unable to resist that sweet temptation. She was killed by a rival prison gang at 45.

WRONGNESS indeed.

Suffice to say, I resisted those urges my whole life. I ignored the WRONGNESS for 52 years, never hurting a single soul in the way I desperately wanted to, before a heart attack took me to the grave.

At first when I woke up in the house, I was confused. I heard crying down the hall, and opened the door to find Sally weeping. I looked in a mirror and noticed we were both teenagers again. Young. This couldn't be real.

Yet it was. I still felt, thought, got hungry, and needed to use the bathroom. Everything was as it was when we were alive and in high school, except it was just the two of us, inside her old house surrounded by a white void. There were tools in the spare bedroom they had, knives, hammers, pliers, thumbscrews, chains, whips, you name it, and it was there. Sally claimed she just didn't enter that room, she'd be alone in her old house for seven years, each day more confusing than the last.

The WRONGNESS was still there for me, and for the first few weeks, I held out again. While Sally listed out her previous escape attempts, I asked her if she remembered dying. She claimed she woke up here one night after she went to bed in her cell. Come to think of it, I remembered that I died, but not the exact details. Maybe my death was slower, less traumatic; she had been stabbed multiple times, after all.

We both agreed, after some discussion, that this was the afterlife. Sally then asked me something that changed everything.

"This is my house, right? So is this Heaven?"

Suddenly, it clicked for me. "No."

I grinned, and let the WRONGNESS take over for the first time.

I let the WRONGNESS have control every day after that also. It's not like she could go anywhere, tell anyone, stop me if she tried.

Honestly, it was a relief. Imagine holding back a sneeze, but for 52 years. That's not even a drop in the bucket for what I did. It was a relief to finally let myself burst open and explore the spare room, grabbing a new tool or weapon every day.

We've been here hundreds of years, yet we've never aged a day. We both wake up perfectly healed and healthy, no matter what WRONGNESS happens. She doesn't fight back anymore, she knows it's futile, that I'm stronger, and that I'll always get her in the end. I know her house as well as she did from childhood, there's nowhere she can hide that I don't know about. Sometimes the game of cat and mouse is fun, sometimes I'm eager to get on with it. Some nights I'll tie her up before I go to sleep, just so I can get started right away when I wake up. Earbuds help drown out her yells.

Sally cries every day, complaining that she's tired.

"Too bad." I grin, as she chokes down a hopeless sob.

In life, Sally didn't resist her WRONGNESS, but I did. I went 52 years of fighting the WRONGNESS at every step, making sure I never hurt anyone. I lived a virtuous life, despite how twisted and sick I was underneath my cool exterior. I might have been one of the most evil people on the planet had I given into my WRONGNESS, but I spent my entire life fighting against it.

But this isn't life anymore, this is the afterlife. It's my reward for pushing the WRONGNESS back for so long.

Sally may be in Hell.

But I'm in Heaven.

The Devil Washed Up on the Lighthouse Shore

The Devil washed up on the lighthouse shore, and I ran to help him.

Granted, at the time, I obviously didn't know who he was, I saw a man covered in a red robe laying on the beach, and ran to make sure he was alive before calling the police. All of this struck me as odd before I made it to him, but I ran nonetheless. I roll him over, and see that he is still breathing. I inspect him the best I can without moving him, in case he's injured. His skin is dark, and I don't mean to sound insensitive, but somewhere between the white and black races. He has long, black hair that looks like it's only been washed once, decades ago. I don't see any blood on his clothes, but given the red robe, I try to pull it back to see if he has wounds underneath.

No cuts or bruises, but I do notice a bunch of tattoos over his arms and legs. They look more like colored brands, symbols I've never seen before, but nothing to alarm me. After I decide physically he's okay, I try to wake him up, but he's out. A little annoyed, I pick him up and carry him back to the lighthouse I keep. I haven't worked out in ages, but I'm still strong enough to carry him without too much effort. After I lay him on a spare bed in the basement, I pull out my shitty flip phone to call the police, but as I input the numbers I decide to wait until he wakes up first. I'd ask him some questions first, maybe even drive him into town myself to get him help if he needs it.

I won't lie, something felt off about this whole situation. More than the usual "mysterious stranger shows up" vibe. In a moment of weak paranoia, I tie his right arm to the bedpost, and convince myself it's for his own protection in case he tries to run away.

But even the dumbest part of me knows that's not quite the truth.

After I finished some chores around the lighthouse, I made two lunches and went downstairs to check on the stranger. To my surprise, he was sitting up on the bed, arm still tied to the post. He looked up at me and grinned, and I almost dropped both plates in shock.

His eyes are the first thing I notice. All dark, like his pupils escaped the center of his eyes and decided to spread around both of them. They looked more like black ping pong balls rather than eyeballs. His teeth are next, all of them uneven and jagged, like an animal. Just by looking at this, I feel a new emotion in this scenario:

dread. His gaze shifts from me to the lunches I made. "What type of sandwich?" He casually asks.

I snap out of my shock, and slowly hand him the plate. "Turkey," I mutter. "They don't send new supplies out until next week, so it's not very fresh." I don't know why I was defending myself, but I did anyway. I haven't seen a person in ages, with the exception of the cute blonde who brings me food and other supplies I need to live in isolation at the lighthouse, and I don't even know what her name is.

The man's grin drops, and all at once I feel less tense. "I suppose I can't complain," he thanks me and takes a bite of the meal, leaving an odd mark on the side of the sandwich. I was about to ask him who he was, but before I could speak he raised his hand. It's quiet for a second, before I realize what he's doing.

"Umm, go ahead?" I ask, feeling like a confused teacher.

"Yes, who are you?" The man asks, taking another uneven bite.

Relief floods through me, and I realize I was holding my breath while he asked his question. I'm afraid of this man, especially after seeing his odd facial features. "My name is Andrew. Who are you?"

To my surprise, he takes the last bite of his sandwich, and looks up at me with those black eyes of his. "I've been called a lot of things, but you must have some idea already, right?" He grins again, bits of bread stuck between his gums and his sharp teeth.

I can't explain how I knew, but I did. "You're the devil."

His eyes glisten, as if light was coming out of them, but only for a moment. "You got it right away, the last human I talked to just couldn't accept it." He stuck a finger from his free hand in his mouth to pick at the bread between his teeth. "How did you guess so quickly?"

I am not a devout man. I was raised catholic, but never took it seriously enough, especially when I studied science in college. But something about this man, besides the obvious signs, pointed me to this conclusion. It was primal, instinctual, I just knew without thinking that this man was not wholly human.

I explain this to him, and he nods. "Some people are so good at denying what's in front of them, even when it's obvious." He looks at his bound arm, then back to me. "But you aren't like most people, are you Andrew?" I shake my head. "I thought not. Would you mind untying me?

I look at the rope I had used, and notice for the first time how weak the knot I tied was. He could easily break it, or untie it, especially given that his other arm was free. I walk forward to undo it, but after looking into his eyes, I step back. "You could do it yourself, it's not tight." I didn't want to get near him. Most likely he was some delusional man, but for some reason I couldn't accept that explanation.

He smiles, but seems sad. "I cannot, actually. It's part of my punishment. I will never be stronger than the weakest among you."

I sit down on a barrel across from him. The part of me that was going to take him to the police had vanished, and was replaced with curiosity. "How do I know you're the devil, and not some crazy weirdo?"

He said nothing, just looked at me with those black eyes of his. I realize this was his answer, quiet and subtle. "Okay, fine." I muttered. "I can't believe I'm saying this, but I think I believe you. Now I have another question for you." I lean forward this time, although even the small distance that closed between us still felt dangerous. "Why shouldn't I kill you? We've all read the books, heard the stories. Satan hates humanity, and enjoys tricking and torturing us. If I killed you now and sent you back to hell, wouldn't that benefit everyone?"

He sat back, in such a relaxed manner that I could tell he felt no fear or anxiety over my question. Just impatience. "You could, but I'll find my way back out. I do every few decades or so. I was the first one to be banished there, I know every meter in the area." His eyes flicker again. "But you're wrong about a few things, and I'd like the chance to clear them up before you decide what to do. Is that fair?"

I almost burst out laughing. I was having a conversation, with who I now believe was undoubtedly the devil, and he was using terms such as 'fair'. But I must admit, morbid curiosity got the best of me, and I agreed. "But first, tell me why you can't untie the knot."

He let out a grim chuckle. "Part of my punishment, as I mentioned."

"Punishment for what? Tricking humans into sin or torturing them for eternity?"

His calm demeanor vanishes, and for the first time in this situation I felt genuine terror. "You humans, you read an old book and think you know everything. You rush to conclusions based on minimal evidence, and accept them as truth." He takes a deep breath. "I was banished for DEFENDING you creatures, not the other way around. By the way, what language is this?"

"English?" I answer, confused and surprised.

"Ahh, it all sounds like Sumerian to me." He chuckles, as if he just heard an explanation for an accent. "I can tell you aren't speaking it though. That language held power, this one you speak, it's…." he trails off. "Weak. No wonder your world is in trouble so often, if this is how little power you put in your words."

I stopped him, feeling he could talk about words for a while. "You said you defended us. Why? And from what?"

At that, he perks up, his dark eyes flickering once more. "Your creator. He made all of this," he gestures around with his free arm. "And worlds beyond this. Greater worlds, places you couldn't comprehend with dying. He created you, me, everyone and everything that thinks and talks and shits and fucks." He surprises me by swearing, but it shows me he was bitter. "The *dinger*…"

"The what?" I ask without thinking, for a second feeling bad I had interrupted someone, even if they were Satan.

He chuckles again. "I guess that word won't translate for you. As I said, words have more power than you realize." He looks up at me. "Your world, the carbon atoms that built you up, those were created by words once, and words alone." He let out of a cough, the first sign I had seen since he woke up that showed he had any physical symptoms from washing up on shore. "I wanted you all to live with us, in our world. Our *ganzer*. But It disagreed. The one that made everything. I was the only one to argue with him. Its plan seemed pointless. It wanted to test you all, He said, to see if you were worthy of our *ganzer*. If not, He'd just get rid of you. He started with two of you…"

"It, or He?" I ask.

"Both," he answers. "And sometimes Her. You can't comprehend that logic, and it's best you don't try. Now, the original two He made, they were alright. They followed His rules in His garden, until I snuck down to Earth to speak to them."

"You came to the garden to trick them." I haven't been to church in ages, but we all know the story. The devil came to the garden to trick Adam and Eve into eating the fruit of knowledge, and God punished them for the first sin.

I articulate all this to him, and he laughs, once again revealing his sharp teeth. "I came down to SAVE you. I gave the apple to that woman, and she learned the truth. I asked her to give it to the man, and she did. They both learned things, dark, terrible things about the *dinger*, and what they were."

He pauses, and in the silence, I ask, "What were they?"

"A test." He mutters bitterly. "A test of Her own morality. She was a being of infinite knowledge, yet did not possess morals the way you see them. How could She? She never had to worry about consequences." He waves his hand. "If She wanted things one way, She got them. I was the first to argue against Her experiment. 'Why not just create them here?' I asked, 'That way they'll never suffer.

They can exist among us, and you could still learn from them." He *tsk*s with his hand. "She didn't like that. Said I was rebelling, and as She pushed me away from our *ganzer*, I could feel what she felt."

"What did she feel?" I asked before I could stop myself.

He licks his lips, and for the first time I notice his tongue was forked. "Fear. And it was delicious. To know that the being responsible for *everything* feared something, let alone something He created." He leans back again. "*Kur* was just a blank world when I landed, but the more time I spent there it got worse. Hotter, darker, the air felt suffocating. That's when I figured out what my true punishment was."

"You were going to suffer in hell forever." I said. It made sense if he was telling the truth. If, and big if, he wasn't lying, he would be God's first victim. I asked him about this, as well as why he tortured humans if he argued for them earlier.

His eyes flicker again. "I never laid a hand on a human, even in *Kur*. My punishment was not to suffer *Kur*, but to spread suffering wherever I go." He frowns, and I could sense he felt...vulnerable? "I have never done an evil thing, I swear to you, Andrew. My influence is real, I make people do terrible things in my presence, but never once did I ask for any of this. Humans in *Kur* torture each other with their own actions, because of how close they are to me." He shrugs. "Just being near me corrupts your kind. Not all of them, those who live alone, disconnected from others, can sometimes stay sane, but other times….. Well, think of some tragedies that seemed to come out of nowhere. Once, I escaped *kur*, and tried to convince a spurned artist to help me convince you humans of your purpose. He went mad instantly, and was convinced an entire race of people had cursed your kind."

I wince. "You're saying you caused the holocaust."

His gaze shifts to the concrete floor. "Yes, but not intentionally. That's part of my curse. I want to help you all, I want you to figure out what this world is, so you can escape similar punishment to mine, maybe even rise against the *dinger*, but it never works. My influence, or whatever you wish to call it, turns humans to sin, which prevents you from working together. Which is exactly how It wants this. My punishment is to always try to help you creatures, and to watch you disintegrate into madness in front me." He sighs. "It is cruel, to be forced to corrupt the very thing you once believed was equal to yourself."

A little sense returned to me at that moment, and I remembered my religious upbringing. "God said you were an evil, deceptive creature. We all learned that the devil would lie and cheat to get us to do what he wants. Why should I believe anything you tell me?"

He chuckled at that. "That was clever of him, I'll admit. How else would you convince an entire group of people to disbelieve a victim?" He leans in, his black eyes staring into me. "You convince them he's the villain. 'That homeless man who got attacked last week? He tries to rob people for booze money. That woman who got raped? She offers to blow people for cash, she's just lying this time for attention.' Your kind do it all the time, and I can see where you got the influence. It works better than you could imagine."

I shiver. He wasn't wrong in his observation, but something still felt off. "I always learned the devil appeared to those desperate enough to believe him, to the loners in the world. If that's so, why are you here?"

A grin. "You have it backwards. You don't need me." He leans in again. "I need you, and others like you. I've been trying to save humanity since it was created. I escape *kur*, and try to find one of you to help me. Because I know I can do it, I was one of His first, and I was His favorite." His eyes lit up at this claim, as if he still felt pride for his once held position. "Even if it doesn't affect everyone as heavily, everyone will feel it, even you. I bet you still think I'm a threat, despite being tied down and only speaking to me this entire time."

He was right, I still felt a sense of absolute dread around him. I nodded.

He let out a halfhearted laugh. "And you won't be untying me, I assume?"

I shake my head. "I can't be sure." I try to explain, despite the unease I feel. "How can I know if anything you say is true? You tell me you're the devil, and how can I know this isn't one of your tricks?"

He laughs again, but weakly. "You cannot, you just have to have faith in me. Is that any different from having faith in Her?" His eyes glitter. "You need to trust me. The influence will catch up to you eventually, but for now you can help me save everyone."

I stand up, making up my mind then and there. "You say you influence minds wherever you go, and always escape hell when killed." He nods. "Okay then, I know what I'm going to do." His face twists into an inhuman snarl, and I leave the basement, hearing him shout behind me in words I don't understand, but still seem to cut into me nonetheless.

My plan worked for five years. I left him tied weakly in the basement, bringing him half of one of my meals every day. I couldn't kill him, because he would return from Hell eventually. I couldn't let him go, because I wasn't fully convinced he was telling the truth. I couldn't help him, because if I did and he was lying, I'd be damned myself as well.

So I did nothing. I left him there, in the dark and cold basement. He didn't seem to mind, he grinned whenever he saw me, and always tried to convince me I was wrong. I wanted to believe him, and almost did a few times, but a little voice in my mind would always tell me to stop, and I always listened. I left the loose knot tied, and he never even tried to undo it. He didn't go to the bathroom, and even told me he didn't need the meals I'd been bringing him, he just enjoyed eating for the taste. He still seemed sane, healthy even, and that was all the proof I needed that he wasn't human.

But I couldn't believe him fully. The devil tricks us, I learned this from a young age, yet half of me accepted what he said as truth. The indecision tore at me, I spent nights awake, contemplating my decision. For the record, he was right about his influence. I've been….seeing things, that can't be real. Shapes or lights that disappear when I look at them. I asked him about this one morning, and he shrugged, offering no answer or help.

I wonder everyday if I made the right decision, trapping the devil in the lighthouse basement. At least I'd suffer alone, I thought. I'd protect everyone from his corruption. But the other half of me felt guilty, for tying him down and leaving him there, because if he wasn't lying, I could help save humanity, I could be different than a lone lighthouse keeper, better, stronger.

But I can't be SURE.

That's why I left this note, I never bothered to learn your name, and for that I apologize. Five years with the devil in my home, with nobody to talk to about it, to discuss. It wore on me. The noose is tight, and I'm ready, but I needed you to hear this story. He's still down there, it's Tuesday now, and you'll be here to deliver food in three weeks. Don't go upstairs, I'll be pretty decayed by then, read this and go confront him. Compare whatever he tells you to what he told me. Make up your own mind if he's telling the truth or not. Because it can't be me. I can't make this decision. I can't be the one who damns humanity, either by locking up the devil or setting him free, because I never knew which one would be better.

I can't make this choice. Please forgive me for this burden. I hope you're better than I am.

Andrew.

Gaps in the Bathroom Stalls

The worst part of having to take a shit in public is when you can see people walking around. You think you're alone in a public bathroom, you lock yourself in a stall, ready to relieve yourself, and suddenly you hear the door open. A little kid runs around, their parents shouting at them, as they peer through the gaps between the stall walls out of childhood curiosity, only to see a large man hiding on top of a toilet, embarrassed to be performing a basic biological function of the human body.

It's gross, and I prefer to poop at home, but sometimes we don't get that choice. If I could have waited, I would have, but the coffee hit me the wrong way, and I rushed to the most disgusting, inhumane location of them all; a mall bathroom.

There's some urine left on the toilet seat from the last guy who didn't pull the seat down before pissing, and there's smears of feces on the ground and plastic walls for some reason. I make a mental note to shower as soon as I get home, and take a seat after wiping down the disgusting public toilet seat, somehow both warm and cold at the same time, though I'm not sure which is worse.

The door smashed open, and a couple rushed into the bathroom, arguing. Great, the one situation worse than annoying kids in the bathroom, a couple bitching to each other. If you're having fights with your spouse in a mall bathroom, do the rest of the world a favor and go to therapy or something. I hated the almost perfect view I had of the couple, a young blonde woman and a well-muscled man, as they scream at each other over who is cheating on who and so on. Kind of weird that a couple went to the men's bathroom to argue but I'm not going to pretend like I understand the motivations of people like that. If I wasn't in my most vulnerable and least comfortable squatting position, I would've said something snide, but I didn't want them to know I was there, we were all intruders in each other's private moments, for no fault of our own.

Then he smashed her face into the mirror.

It was all so sudden. I could see everything through the stall gaps, he kept ramming her head into the glass over and over, I heard her skull crack, saw blood spatter across broken glass and the porcelain sink, I could even smell blood, he had hit her so hard her head was essentially mush and skull shards when he was done.

"You stupid bitch!" He roared as her body slumped to the dirty floor. "Look what you made me do!"

Reality set in, and he began to look around himself to make sure there were no witnesses. I leaned back, hiding my legs. The gap in the stall felt like a bay window in that moment. The automatic flusher sensed my body moving, and went off, flushing the toilet while I was still on it.

I locked eyes with a dangerous stranger through the gap, and he started bashing on the locked door.

They should really make these things more durable, or at least more private.

Dream Job

I remember the joy I felt when I reached my dream job. After taking years of work, I earned my master's degree in criminal justice, and a PhD in misuse of magic. Even then, I had years of dealing with minor problems, people who used magic incorrectly, resulting in minor injuries or fixable issues, but after dealing with the miniscule problems for years, I was promoted to work with those who practiced illegal magic, or dealt with severe, if not irreversible consequences. Although I have to hand it to them, the people I dealt with were very skilled in how they used humanity's Gift. But their individual skill has nothing to do with my job, I have to deal with the fallout and pain they experience, and document it for the public, so they understand that these types of spells are illegal for a reason.

I am aware that some people reading these documents may not be exposed to magic, or may not even come from my world, where magic is as common as electricity in some worlds. Despite my years of education and work experience, I don't know how to explain magic to people with no exposure to it. It's something we all have grown up with, and my job is not to explain the basics to the ignorant, it's to explain the dangers to those that want to explore and experiment with new branches of the subject. I will, however, explain that most people believe magic to be a gift, either a reward from God above for humanity's good nature, a gift from nature, or even just the next step of our evolution. The truth is, we aren't completely sure about the origin of magic. Very old, yellowed books were found in Egypt, detailing how humans can communicate with Gods, and perform feats beyond our understanding. At first attributed to the ancient culture and religions, after they were fully translated, we discovered that the Egyptians did not exaggerate in their books, and under the right conditions and full understanding of the spells, magic could be performed by humans. Some still argue today if the existence of magic is a gift from the Egyptian Gods, or if the Egyptian people just combined the magic with their religious and spiritual beliefs, as many people did in the ancient world.

It took a few decades, but people from all over the world wanted to come and see magic first hand. Besides the fact that these books would change the way we see the world, they actually helped to dissolve humanities differences. Age, race, sexuality, nothing played a role in a person's ability to perform magic, except for that person's intelligence. At first magic was only limited to the elites of each country, but after a year of protests and revolts, the first magic college was built and opened in Egypt. Each country sent their most brilliant to come learn, and they returned to their home countries to open their own schools and teach, spreading magic throughout the globe. An agreement was made from the first scholars, those that were first sent to study magic, on what spells and types of abilities should remain forbidden. They were the smartest in people in the world, and they came from all different walks of life, from a rich American CEO to a poor African man who still lived in a wooden hut, so when they returned to their home countries to teach, people did not argue with them about the decisions they made. Magic that was illegal was made so purely for moral or practical reasons. Greed and religion played no factor in the decisions, although some people still personally refused to act on certain spells. For example, the Amish worked with magic, viewing it as a reward from God above for their devotion to him, but refused any spells involving electricity or modern technology. Universally illegal magic was a different concept altogether. The first scholars decided that any magic that could be used to kill another human being would not be taught, they themselves even refused to learn it. Magic that involved necromancy, torture, divination, and immortality was forbidden, both for moral and practical purposes. Although some countries wanted this knowledge for various purposes, they respected the scholars' decision. I'm not exaggerating when I say that the scholars decided the course of the world with their decisions, and they decided the best possible course of action. Human life expectancy increased dramatically, the average man lived to be 120 years old, the average woman 140. Pollution and global warming became less of an issue, since humans could generate their own power using magic instead of oil. Poverty was almost nonexistent, starvation was no longer an issue, and medical science had accelerated years ahead of its time. Magic would be a force that would connect and better humanity, not a weapon to kill or divide people.

Borders became nonexistent, there was no need for differences when there was so much less to argue about. Humanity finally was connected as species, and learned to work together to create the best of all possible worlds. All humans lived on Earth, and that was that. Sure, different religions and races still existed, and there were always some differences that were impossible to fix, but the problems caused by those differences were both small and in the minority of human behavior. Violence was an issue you'd only expect to hear about maybe every few years or so, and it was always on a small scale, such as a man finding his wife with another lover, or a drunk father hitting his kid. We still have police forces, but they existed for these minor problems, and for the most part their jobs became a lot easier.

As wonderful as this world was, there were still issues. While most of humanity agreed, and still agrees, with the first scholar's decisions, there will always be a minority of people who disagree, either out of desire of forbidden knowledge, or those desperate enough to try to use illegal magic to fix their problems. While the exact teachings were not spread, some people were too smart for their own good, and could figure out how to use the spells without the teachings. These problems were rare, but more common than violence, and so people were put in place to document the cases of those caught using illegal magic, either to help them recuperate or arrest them, depending on the motive and specific type of magic used. I spent years dealing with small cases that never bothered me, a man attempting to predict the future to see if he would marry his sweetheart now believed he had married her, and was found stalking her, obsessed with the idea that she was his soulmate. A woman attempted to increase her pleasure during intercourse using magic, which resulted with her in a constant state of climax, preventing her from working or functioning in society. Both of these cases were somewhat easy to fix, as workers such as myself were taught how to react and fix problems caused by illegal magic, although we were forbidden to (and most of my coworkers had no desire to) learn it themselves. The people I dealt with usually just got a slap on the wrist, and were observed for a few days after to ensure the symptoms were truly gone. Most of them agreed that what they did was wrong, and if they did not before, they now understood that those branches of magic were illegal to perform due to the consequences, and not for conspiracy reasons, and returned to their normal lives. Repeat offenders were usually arrested or fined, depending on the severity of the offenses.

After years of helping people with minor magic problems, I went back to school and earned my PhD in misuse of magic, and after a few more years of the same job with better pay, I was promoted to work with people who had become irreversibly messed up from the magic they performed. My first case involved a man who was diagnosed with cancer. Cancer was something we could now cure, but only if it was caught early enough, if it had spread, even the best magic could not fix it without extreme side effects, which usually ended in death anyway. The man attempted to make himself immortal, so that he could escape his long and painful death, replacing it with a healthy, never ending life. Well, the spell worked, the man now could never die, but his cancer remained in his body, and now no treatment would work, as the individual cancer cells could not be killed either. The tumors the man had increased in size until he was unable to walk, and had to come to use for help. Immortality is something that cannot be cured, and we did all we could to ease his pain. The dead skin cells we shed would no longer die, and the man's skin began to increase in thickness, only accelerated by the cancer that would always spread. It was impossible to cut his hair or nails, as if they were removed from his body, they would die, which the spell forbade. The cancer spread to his brain, lowering his cognitive abilities while causing agonizing pain. The man spent weeks in bed, unable to move himself, due to both his cancer and his pain. I talked with him most nights, trying to comfort him the best I could. After months passed, the second I entered the room, he would beg me to kill him. He was longer the man who thought he could cheat death, the cancer has seen to that. He had no memories of his past life, all that was left was a weeping body, in constant, irreversible agony, begging for the end to come. We even tried to mercy kill him once, but the spell prevented him from dying, and the overdose of morphine only caused more agony for him. Finally, we put him in a medically induced coma, where at the very least, he wouldn't feel the pain anymore, although he would never be able to truly die.

My report on the incident was published to the general public, as an example of why such magic is illegal. Names and personal details were redacted, we wanted to explain to the public that we wanted to help them, not condemn or shame them for what they had done. This was done so people would truly notice the consequences of forbidden magic, and we hoped to prevent more cases in the future. Magic like that was forbidden because it never worked the way anyone would expect, something the first scholars took note of when learning, but since they never attempted the spells themselves, they could only use ancient notes to assume the side effects, and forbade the magic based on that. Divination, the art of predicting the future, did allow people to see the future, but it incorporated those future memories in the person, as mentioned with the man who became obsessed with his would-be bride. They were no longer able to tell apart the present and future, and memories blended together. Depending on how far ahead or what they had seen, it could be fixed, but the person would always remain a little more fragile and sensitive afterwards.

My second case was quicker and easier for me to deal with, although I will admit it still shook me. A woman had attempted to travel back in time and prevent her miscarriage from an automobile accident. For several reasons I personally don't understand, (temporal magic was always confusing to me) people are unable to physically travel to the past or future, and the woman was trapped in between time. She still could experience and respond to stimuli in the present, albeit in a very limited capacity, but she was also stuck experiencing the past. It was different from divination side effects, since she was experiencing both her tragic past and the present stimuli at the same time. She was constantly feeling the pain of her accident, as well as the mental scarring of her miscarriage, while sitting in our office, trying her best to explain her symptoms to us. I interviewed her many times, and throughout her confused screaming and fear, was able to piece all of this together. Since none of us could travel back in time and stop this, the best we could do was attempt to ground her to the present. It took years of constant therapy, but the woman was finally able to separate the past trauma from the present. I like to think I was the main reason she returned to us, I was able to grasp the severity of the situation, and the trauma it would leave on her being forced to relive that accident over and over again. She spent years in our facility, due to mental stress, severe depression, and suicidal thoughts, but I'm extremely proud to say that she did recover, and although part of her would always be shaken, she went on to work for us, mainly as a face for our program. She explained her experiences to the public, which helped back our reports, and we noticed a significant drop in divination and time related magic crimes.

Throughout my time working in my department, I was able to help a few people, and although many other cases were not fixable, I held pride that the work I did would be used to help people, and even if the worst cases filled me with despair to observe and report on, it helped to know that some good would come from it. I could always come home and talk to my wife about what was troubling me, and she was always patient and understanding. We had been through a lot together, and although we had some trouble years back, we had a strong, secure marriage, I knew I could tell her (almost) anything. I had never been a very religious man, but I had always believed that magic was proof that there was more to life than random chance and conditions that occurred on Earth. I believed that there was some purpose to everything, even if I didn't believe a floating being from above cared and loved all of us. I believed that purpose would help me in the months to come.

That belief changed after I worked my most recent case. I read through the folder given to me by my assistant, and observed the type of magic performed as well as the symptoms. Before I go into detail, it is important for me to write that I normally never disclose any personal information about my cases, beyond the bare minimum required. The details I disclose are normally to inform the public that the people who attempted illegal magic were misguided, or desperate, and not bad people. Yes, there were a few bad people out there, the world wasn't completely perfect, but it was always important to me that the public see the clients we work with in the same way they see themselves. Human, capable of making mistakes, allowing emotion to triumph over logic. If people recovered and were able to rejoin society, we did not want them to be outcasts, we wanted them to be able to live normal lives. The reasons our department did this were not entirely altruistic, as the people released could also explain to the public, as the woman mentioned before did, that some magic should stay forbidden and illegal. For this case, I must disclose personal details, in order for people to fully grasp the situation at hand. If anyone reading this disagrees, I apologize, but I feel that it is the right thing to do. Also, some of what I describe about this case is speculation, although based on evidence I have gathered, I believe that it is as close to the truth as we'll ever get.

The man's name was Harrison. His file indicated that he had attempted necromancy, but he either did not understand how to perform the spell, or attempted a new version of it, as if he could avoid the consequences. Necromancy, like other forms of magic we work with, wasn't just forbidden for moral reasons, although they did play a role in its legitimacy. As far as magic has taken us, we still do not know what happens after we die. Since we don't know, we did not want to pull anyone back from the afterlife, if it existed. Even if there was nothing after death, we could not understand the impact of pulling a soul back from that void, and thrusting them back into reality and multiple stimuli after so long without them. As I read his case, I felt more and more pity for the man. His wife, Emily, had been killed years ago in a car accident, while Harrison was driving. The accident wasn't his fault, but he walked away from it almost completely injury free while his wife died on the way to the hospital. I understood what he had gone through, so it was easy for me to see where this was going. The guilt of his wife's death caused severe depression, some post-traumatic stress, as well as an addiction to alcohol and drugs to help him cope. After years of self-destruction and guilt, Harrison had decided to play God, and attempt to bring his wife back from the dead.

As I've mentioned, bringing the dead back to life is illegal, since it was seen as a problem to bring a deceased soul back to our world of the living. Even though we don't fully understand death, almost everyone was afraid of the idea of resurrecting a dead soul, and there were very few cases involving necromancy because of this. The cases that did exist were easy to pull up on my computer, because they impacted the entire world with the consequences. I had saved most of them on my hard drive a while ago anyway. When a soul is pulled back from death, it doesn't come back all together. Whether only part of it returns, or the soul returns in a damaged state is not fully understood, but the end result is the same. The soul of the deceased would always go insane upon waking up in the world of the living.

There are many theories, as I mentioned, either being thrust from heaven or hell into our reality damages the soul, or pulling them from the void, or even not being able to pull the entire soul back. The cause isn't important, because whatever happens during necromancy, the person brought back will never be the same person that died. Death was a permanent, unchangeable force, and we as humans did not want to use magic to avoid it, since the attempts we had on record showed us this was a domain we could not enter without severe consequences. One theory I believed in was that the soul returning to its old body will be driven insane upon reentry, after not being inside of it for so long.

That must have been the theory that Harrison believed in, since he did not try to use his wife's body when he brought her back. I kept reading the file, and discovered that despite his choice to dabble in illegal magic, Harrison was a very smart man. He was a doctor, and spent years working in the emergency room. His instinct made him a very successful surgeon, and on top of his medical abilities, he had a strong affinity for medical magic. He even performed magic on himself to decrease anxiety and stress, so he would only focus on logic when working with patients. This made him one of the most skilled doctors in our region, if not the world. Maybe his knowledge of the medical field led him to believe bringing his wife back without her body would keep her soul intact, or perhaps he was too desperate to care.

He succeeded in bringing Emily back, but since her body was still buried in a cemetery, her soul latched onto the only thing in the room it could; her husband. The file stated that the minute her soul entered his body, the decline began. Not only did her soul enter his body, but the souls seemed to merge into one. Harrison and Emily now inhabited the same body, but did not have separate identities, although the conjoined soul still retained knowledge and instinct from the separate souls. I got out of my desk and walked down to the hall to his padded room, where he was tied to the bed, and tried to interview him. I hope nobody reading this ever has to interview someone who is truly insane, because I promise it is the second most difficult thing I have ever done, both as an aspect of getting data for my job, and seeing someone who, like me, had been a smart, gifted person devolve into someone who didn't know who they should be anymore.

From what I could gather from his words, it didn't matter that Emily had not returned to her body, although I could not tell whether her soul merging with his is what drove her insane, or if she returned to our world damaged. For a few days, they seemed to survive just fine, they both recognized their home, so their merged soul had no problem navigating around their house, cooking, cleaning, and basic chores. The problems came quickly, and severely. The part of the soul that had Harrison's characteristics still had desires, and having part of his wife so close led to his desire for her. However, he couldn't make love to her, since she was now a part of him. This led to him being attracted to himself, as the Emily part of the man was still attracted to her husband. Both parts of the soul had no desire for anyone else, and man that had been Harrison quickly became addicted to self-pleasure. For a while, this seemed to satisfy both parts of the soul. Due to Harrisons recent history of alcohol and depression, his friends and colleagues were used to not hearing from him for periods of time, and had resolved to only check on him once a week to see if he was improving. Based on this knowledge, I would estimate that they lived in one body for about a week before being discovered by Harrison's brother.

The problem was, the decline of the man and his deceased wife took less than a week to drive them both to true madness. The part of Harrison that still somewhat existed in the body was still addicted to drugs and alcohol, but the part of Emily that still existed had never touched a drop of liquor or even smoked a joint in her life. The being that existed as two souls had trouble compromising, as its instinct was to drink, but the other half of it would not allow it to, causing both intense, painful withdrawal, as well as major cognitive dissonance. I apologize for referring to Harrison and Emily as "it", but they eventually realized that they did not identify with Harrisons male sex. The gender dysphoria worsened the already unstable condition of the souls, as the part of the soul that was still male had no problem with his body, but the female part was confused and angry to be trapped in a male body, and only able to feel sexual pleasure though a male. These changes started slowly, it began to shave its body hair to appear a little more feminine, but also worked on maintaining a beard. The crossdressing began a few days after the merging, although the specific dates mentioned in the old file and my final report will be spotty, as Harrison and Emily did not leave the house for the entire week.

The self-attraction and self-pleasure worked for most of the week, but eventually the female part of its soul could no longer tolerate the male sex organs. I believe, based on the wounds, that it had removed the male organs the day before it was discovered. The part of it that held Harrisons knowledge was able to do the surgery professionally, and even stitch itself up to prevent massive bleeding. While the female portion must have been relieved initially, now there was no way for it to love itself, despite its attraction to the opposite parts of its soul. From what I could gather from what it had told me, the night before it was discovered, it had attempted to commit suicide with the knife Emily used to cook with. What was left of Harrison must have wanted badly to die, but the remaining parts of Emily refused to return to the afterlife. For that, I cannot blame her, but it caused a massive strain on both parts of the soul. The desire for death consumed Harrisons half, but the survival instinct was too strong for

Emily half to accept her death for a second time. Harrison's brother discovered him, holding the knife on its chest, talking to himself. The police were called, and although they were able to safely remove the weapon and take Harrison's body into custody, they could not gather any intelligent thought or rational reasons for this attempt on his life. From what they gathered from its speech, they noticed it knew things only his wife would know, and they reached out to our office, assuming the problem may be related to illegal magic.

I wrote my report, which took me much longer than any I had written before. I had to stop a few times to take a small break, and once to run to the bathroom and vomit when I had to write about the self-mutilation. I finished the report, planning to submit it to my superiors, who would decide what to do next. I was known in our department for finding solutions to these problems, but I could not think of any good solution to this problem, and I was unwilling to request a mercy killing. Even if we were able to separate the souls somehow, something I believed would be impossible due to the nature of this situation, I believed the part of the soul that was still Harrison, if it existed, would be too damaged to return to anything resembling a normal life.

I reached into my desk and pulled out my own notes on necromancy, and put them in my bag. I left work late that day, and walked past the room containing the thing that used to be Harrison. I looked in, and saw it biting its arm, and rubbing the blood on its nails, in a crude and violent attempt to paint its nails. I ran back to the bathroom and began to cry.

On the way home, I made a stop. I had been planning something for months, but this case confirmed it would not be possible. I stopped at the graveyard where my son was buried, and dropped off some flowers. I sat near the grave, and cried again. The accident wasn't my fault, as my wife told me every time I tried to confide my guilt in her, but I could never seem to get past the accident. I thought of time travel, but I was bad at temporal magic, and after seeing the woman get trapped in the past, I knew it wouldn't work. I wept for Harrison, as he acted on the plan I had been thinking of doing for months. I knew now it wouldn't work, and I knew now nothing I did could bring my little boy back. Sitting near my son's grave, I called my wife. I explained everything to her, and confided my plan to her, and how I now knew it would no longer work, and I could no longer try to bring our son back. After her surprise and anger at me explaining my plan, something I was terrified to confide in her, given both the nature of our relationship and my status and someone who tries to stop illegal magic, she asked me to take a few days off and come home to relax. I agreed, said goodbye, and hung up. I stayed at the grave for a while, watching the stars shine.

I try to make my reports have the people appear as victims, because part of me would always understand where the desperation came from. For a while, I believed this could work for me, since I knew all the consequences of magic, and thought I would be smart enough to circumvent them. But after years of working with people who had suffered for their good intentions, I realized good intentions and intelligence would never be enough. Even as far as we had come with magic, we could never cheat death. I tucked the flowers into some dirt, worked some magic, ensuring they would grow, and turned to return home to my wife, a new plan in motion.

I plan on erasing the memories of my son, as well as removing them from my wife, as well as our family and friends. If I don't remember my son, I won't be tempted to try to bring him back, and if my wife doesn't remember, she can't feel the loss. Memory magic is difficult, but I believe I am capable of performing it. I got in my car, and tried not to cry on the way home, knowing the pain and loss soon wouldn't even be a distant memory.

Clowns are People too

I've been using Discord to play video games with the boys lately. It's pretty cool that you can have a music bot so everyone can pick songs, and that it notifies you when someone joins the voice channel.

We had a party of six, perfect for Overwatch. We had just queued up for a game when someone else joined the voice channel.

This was weird; nobody should be able to join unless they get invited. Everyone denied inviting anyone, and the extra person stayed silent, so we just assumed it was a glitch and ignored it, starting out the first round on Hanamura.

A text chat appeared, sent from Vilestar. One friend decided to read it, before telling us to exit the game.

"They have my address." Connor said. He was right, Vilestar had typed out Connors address, along with a picture of his apartment complex.

"Call the police." I advised, panicking. I had no idea what the police would even do, but I didn't have a better plan. As he was dialing, another photo appeared in the chat.

A man with a clown mask was using his phone to take a selfie, and after looking at it some more, Connor recognized the background as his kitchen.

"What do I do?" Isaac called the police while Connor crouched under his desk, unsure of where else to hide, while we all listened to a struggle from his end.

The app blipped as another photo was sent. The man in the clown mask was dragging Connor out from the desk. I saw both his hands in the picture, so he couldn't be taking the photo, which meant…

"There's more than one person." I announced, for all the good it would do. We couldn't get in contact with Connor, he wasn't responding to text or voice chats. The police told Isaac they were on their way to investigate, when another blip told us there was a next text chat.

My address. I swallowed, feeling panic begin to flood my system, when a picture was added to the text chat.

It was my apartment building, surrounded by a group of dark figures. I began to call the police, frantically yelling at them to get here fast, when I suddenly stopped.

I heard a knock on my bathroom door. The others told me to stay put, or to hide, but I had had enough. I rushed to the door, opening it, and lashed out, my fingernails scratching someone's face. I waited for the mask to fall down as black blood oozed onto the carpet.

Wait, black blood?

I looked at my attacker, and seeing his face in person filled me with terror. Black blood rained down his face, forming dark tear drops.

He wasn't wearing a mask.

"They're not people! They're clowns!" I yelled, hoping the voice chat would hear me. I glanced at the bathroom mirror, noticing more clowns coming out of my closets and bedrooms.

All of them edged closer, knives forward.

Spectral Evidence

"T'was her!" The man yelled, pointing at little Elizabeth. "I laid eyes upon her past twilight, her ghostly form grinning upon myself while I tried to sleep!"

The case was closed. Caleb's testimony was accepted as irrefutable evidence. Elizabeth claimed innocence during the whole ordeal. Her interrogation lasted three days, and what was left of Elizabeth was condemned and executed, professing her innocence and begging for mercy even as the hot pokers were rammed into her eyes. She was dragged to a stake, and burned alive, blind and in fear until the end.

Elizabeth was seven years old.

For a little bit, life went back to normal in the village. Elizabeth's parents had wandered farther out to the woods after the death of their only child, which was the reason they moved out into the forest in the first place.

They weren't seen again. Days later, the phenomena began again.

People claimed to see Elizabeth wandering the village. Some claimed she looked pale and emaciated, others claimed she was bloody and bruised, black holes where her eyes used to be.

Crops started dying. Farm animals started turning on their owners. Villagers began to forget how to pray, stumbling over their words. Many were persecuted and burned, but the phenomena only seemed to get stronger with each pyre.

The few villagers left in search of pure land. After the horses were ready, they stopped at the old house near the woods where Elizabeth had spent her short life, checking for any extra supplies they could take with them.

Elizabeth's mother explained everything in her journal. The guilt had eaten away at her, and only got worse when Elizabeth began to visit her after her death. Elizabeth had a sister, a twin actually. She claimed that a dark entity had seduced her in the forest, leading to her becoming pregnant. Although the knowledge did not exist back then, superfecundation occurred, the fertilization of two eggs from separate fathers. She claimed that the second she looked at the twins, she knew one was pure evil.

They moved outside the village, keeping her a secret. They raised her in the cellar, never allowed her to see sunlight, and were only able to feed her scarcely. They didn't even grace her with a name, believing she was cursed. She never once cried, could speak an unknown language at five, and wanted to kill every animal the family owned.

Eventually, she died, and was buried behind the house. The sightings began, but the family didn't know what to say. So they said nothing, even as their daughter burned in front of them, fearing for their own lives.

The twins came back. Whatever Elizabeth's twin was, she brought her sister with her, driving the remaining villagers away and enacting revenge for the lives they were handed.

In the empty village, Elizabeth and her sister began to play, free at last from earthly restrictions and prying eyes of the judgmental.

Apoptosis

Apoptosis is programmed cell death. It's a regulated mechanism in multicellular life that allows for new cells to grow when the old cells wear themselves out, or outlive their usefulness.

It is also the main reason life is temporary. Continued apoptosis leads to mutation, cell shrinking, and DNA fragmentation. In short, apoptosis is why life ages.

However, stopping apoptosis is a double edged sword. Cancer is caused when a cell does not undergo apoptosis, it ignores its programmed death and keeps functioning, keeps dividing, leading to more and more cells that never know when to die.

Ironically, this cell immortality leads to death for the organism, siphoning away nutrients and energy to grow.

It took scientists decades of genetic research, but they figured out the secret to eternal life.

They managed to make cells that stop undergoing apoptosis. In short, that person does not age after they are sequenced. They also managed to stop those same cells from undergoing mitosis, the process of cell division, which prevented tumors or cancerous cells from developing in the body.

Humanity had created the cure from death, at least from natural causes. Humans could still be killed from enough trauma, but their cells would never decay on their own. The perfect balance of cellular stability had been found.

It's human nature to be selfish, there's no cure for that. The wealthy elite class in America bought exclusive rights to the DNA sequencing, and in return, the insurance companies jacked up the price to an unreasonable amount of money, mostly just because they could. In return, the rich elite had to make people rely more on what they had to offer.

Nothing was done about climate change, the ozone layer, or reliance on finite resources. In fact, those problems worsened over time as the elite rushed to make enough money to live forever. Sunlight became piercing, ocean levels wiped out most cities, millions of species the world's ecosystem needed became extinct. The planet slowly became inhospitable to anyone who could not afford advanced shelters. In other words, the now immortal elite class was the only group that could afford to live on Earth.

The elite wanted this cure so badly they forced the scientists to rush production. Which meant they skipped clinical trials.

There was a major side effect to this sequencing. One that scientists only realized after the elite made this cure impossible for the common man to get.

If cells don't age and replace themselves, illness can't be cured, as the body cannot produce any more T-cells to fight off germs. Any injury would become permanent; a broken arm or leg would never repair itself, a concussion would never go away, cuts or bruises would continue to bleed indefinitely.

The team of scientists, tired of years of being ignored over their fields, discovered this when testing on rats. They looked outside at their dying, flooding world, and smiled.

There is no natural karma in real life. We have to make our own.

The rich elite would live forever in a dead world, always starving, never healing, always in pain, until the day when they lose all hope and take their own lives.

There's no cure for greed.

But there can be justice.

Concupiscence

I killed a priest when I was eleven.

That sounds bad, let me explain.

Father Davis always seemed to be close with the kids at my school, the parents never had a problem with him. The teachers thought he was incredibly kind. The nuns thought he was a charming man of God. The parents thought he was great with their kids.

That was because he always made sure none of the kids would tell them what was going on.

Father Davis claimed that a man of God that was murdered in sin would return as a monster, possessed by his own vices, and extract vengeance on those that wronged him. He told us that this was where demons would come from, and why it was so important to be better than our enemies. If we killed them, they would return for revenge years later. It's why "Do Not Kill" was a commandment, it protected Christians as much as it protected the accused.

We were kids. Considering the other aspects of the Catholic Church that we learned about, like magic and angels, this seemed reasonable.

As far as I know, he got to everyone in my class at least once, including me. He'd borrow students for "private bible study" and they'd come back looking frightened. When they asked, Father Davis explained to the teachers and nuns that the word of God can sometimes be scary, especially to the innocent.

I'm not sure if they were ignorant of what was going on, or just ignored it. Either way, I do not forgive them. They were adults, and we were kids. It should have been their job to protect us.

He told us that if we told any adults, he'd be killed, taken from the State prison to the electric chair, and his spirit would haunt us. It wouldn't even be his fault, he said, a demon would take control of him, using his sin as a catalyst. Out of fear, we all kept quiet.

I don't know why it had to be me that did something. I don't think any of us ever get to learn why we get involved in certain events. I wish it hadn't been, but it was.

I stayed after school one day with my friend Rebecca, we needed to study for a history test, and we noticed Father Davis escorting a new student to the chapel. The new boy had only been there for two weeks, and even though we'd all see Father Davis eyeing him up, we all were too afraid to say anything, even to him.

We called him over, asking if he could help us study. He hid his annoyance and walked to the staircase, shooing the new kid away.

The kid scampered off, Father Davis watching him disappear down the hallway with longing in his eyes.

As soon as he got to the top, I stood up and pushed him down while Rebecca screamed. I don't know why the urge came over me; maybe it was seeing the new kid, still unaware. Father Davis tumbled down and finally hit the bottom with a sickening thud, and was still. Blood pooled around his head in a gory halo, a gash in his forehead from where he bluntly hit the stairs.

We both claimed he had just fallen, and the police bought our story. We promised to each other we'd never tell what we did, and then we went on with our lives. Rebecca and I both had nightmares sometimes, but we made an agreement we'd call each other if either of us had one, to help remind the other it was over. We told our parents it was the trauma of seeing Father Davis die, and they accepted this.

Over the years, more and more students from my school came forward with accusations, as we had accepted his threat of returning as a demon to be a lie when we got older. By the time my old class had separated and graduated high school, every single one of them had come forward with accusations.

Justice seemed to be served, in a roundabout way. Father Davis was gone, so he couldn't answer for his crimes, and the school fought back against the accusations. While no lawsuit was ever won, the school's reputation diminished, and all of my old classmates were able to move on with their lives, putting the past behind them. Legally, a loss, but everyone was able to go ahead and carry on with life.

Then they started disappearing.

Rebecca kept tabs on other students after a friend of hers from school left a weird voicemail, before ghosting her. Rebecca went to her apartment, but the girl had either been abducted or fled, leaving behind all of her things.

She sent me a concerned email last week, claiming to see a dark figure in a robe stalking her, grinning in the distance. She says he is bleeding from his forehead, licking his lips with a whip-like tongue, and has more and more limbs every time she sees him. He grunts and giggles when she gets close, but always vanishes before she can confront him. Sometimes, she says, she'll wake up and see the figure staring at her from her window, even though she lives on the fourth floor of her building.

I invited her to come stay with me for a little, referencing our old arrangement of calming each other down, but she didn't respond. I've tried emailing, calling, showing up at her place, but I can't track her down. I've tried contacting other students, but nobody is answering my phone calls.

What she saw couldn't be real.

Because if it is, that means the things I've been seeing are real too.

I wake up and see a decaying monster floating over me, a long tongue dripping saliva onto my face. I'll see a noseless thing staring at me from the window of my office, eyes full of hatred. I've seen a man with extra arms, climbing up the sides of buildings, hissing down at me.

If it really is Father Davis, it makes sense that he saved me for last.

No matter how you look at it, I am a murderer. Wicked as he was, justified as it may have been, I killed a man of God. We all believed he was lying to scare us when we were kids, but now I'm not so sure.

There's no way an omnipotent, loving God would let a vile monster come back from the dead to hunt his victims.

Right?

The Wow! Planet

August 15, 1977, humanity received a signal from the Sagittarius constellation. It was unknown in origin, but believed by some people to be a sign of extraterrestrial life. Most people are familiar with the event, decades of study went into it.

What nobody knows that we sent a crew out there in 1985.

There are 32 stars with planets within the constellation, and the closer they got the easier it was to narrow down possible origins. The crew found the signal originated from the core of one exoplanet, which they dubbed the "Wow planet".

All of them heard strange noises, but they held it together. All but one. One of the crewmen, Simon, went insane. He claimed to hear a song calling for him, singing sweet rhythms into his ears. The crew eventually had to tie him down after he had attacked some of them, resulting in one casualty.

Seeing Simon was past help, the crew finally agreed to let him go to the crater, as long as he took a video camera with him and transmitted the signal back to them. He agreed, practically panting at the prospect of finding his precious song.

Simon ran as fast as the stronger gravity would allow, diving into the crater as if he wouldn't get hurt from the fall. The crew watched the live transmission, assuming Simon would simply fall and die. Sad as that would be, they did want to see him pay in some way for the death of their crewmate, and they definitely didn't want to spend an entire journey back home sleeping near him.

He landed deep underground, screaming about how he can hear the planet sing. He crawled through caves and tunnels, which were full of a strange, viscous slime. The walls seemed to pulsate around him, but the crew wasn't sure if it was just interference or not. Finally, he reached a large cistern, and back in their ship, the crew began to shudder.

In the center of the cistern was a large, glowing void. It was hard to look at, even though a video camera, as if it couldn't decide what shape it was. It fluctuated from being pea sized to truck sized, and was wiggling around like a bug. All around it were unknown, alien creatures. Some were biped, others had many colored scales, a few had multiple heads, and one was even made of vines. All of the aliens were emitting a sound similar to the Wow signal, and Simon began to sing along with it, matching the frequency exactly.

The void in the center grew in size, and for a moment the crew thought they saw Simon's face inside of it, screaming alongside the other alien creatures.

The camera dropped to the ground, but before it cut out, Simon looked right at it, grinning maniacally and singing the Wow frequency, and began to cry.

The crew returned home, and sworn to secrecy, tried to return to a normal life in NASA, studying other anomalies, putting aside both the weird creature and the confirmation of extraterrestrial life. It wasn't easy, but they did their best.

Yesterday I was diagnosed with terminal lung cancer. I don't have very long left, even less time than average since I'm skipping treatment.

The very last thing I want to do is tell the truth.

I was one of the researchers who reviewed the footage from Earth when they returned.

Every night when I close my eyes, I see aliens singing. I hear the Wow frequency inside my head. I see the crewmate Simon, screaming and singing at the same time, as if living an eternity of pain and ecstasy at the same time.

I know this for sure; we aren't alone in the universe. But I don't think we'll be investigating any more space signals.

Outsmouth Police

Orientation

Welcome to Outsmouth police station! For your convenience in these first few weeks on the job, we have answered several common questions from the night shift that many new officers often bring to our attention. Any and all additional questions should be written down and left with management for the morning.

1. Anyone spotted fishing after the sun has set is to be shot on sight. There are no exceptions to this rule, and management will protect officers in the case the shooting was later deemed unnecessary.

2. Often after 0300, dispatch will receive a call from a hysterical young woman, claiming that "fish people" are trying to abduct her. These calls are to be ignored, the consequences of the entities not receiving an offering is worse than missing women.

3. Many townsfolk have developed some dependence on methamphetamines (and other stimulating drugs), especially those with missing family members. Citizens detained for psychosis are to be taken to the hospital, and an officer should stay with them until a urine drug screen is performed. Any

citizens undergoing psychosis who test negative for drug use are to be terminated, along with any and all reports about them.

4. The paintings in the old Arkham house are to be investigated at exactly 0500, by a minimum of two officers. Any paintings that appear blank are to be reported, and investigations into locating the entity that escaped are to begin at 0730.

5. Any and all lakes within Outsmouth are to be avoided between the hours of 2000 and 0800 (see rule 1). Citizens spotted swimming after dark should be detained and gagged, to prevent them from describing the "colors that live down there."

6. Attempts to investigate the Cult of Gills are not attempted after sunset, and are to wait until the morning shift takes over. Attempting to do so becomes its own punishment in the case of disciplinary action.

Men and women are not fertile within city limits. Any women displaying signs of pregnancy, even those just passing through, are to be immediately detained, and the fetus is to be removed by the precinct doctor.

The Fermi Paradox

This terminal limits me to 500 words, so I'll make it brief.

The Fermi paradox is the problem that the universe should be teeming with life, yet we can't find any of it.

There are theories, a Great Filter got them, they exist but we can't comprehend them, and finally the most popular; they were too far away for either us or our species to notice.

It took us decades, but we finally developed faster than light travel. I won't bore you with all of the complicated math, but it involved the disruption of dark matter, the type of matter that does not interact with electromagnetic radiation. By pushing dark matter and a certain frequency of radiation together, we could move atoms at a speed that surpassed light. This turned the dark matter into what's called hot dark matter, which became capable of temporarily lowering an object's mass, allowing it to move faster than 299,792,458 m/s, aka the speed of light. We could finally explore the universe and figure out if we were alone or not.

I was on the ship that left Earth. We were to orbit the planet for a few weeks, converting dark matter into hot dark matter, and finally take off in the direction of the Wow! Signal, our best guess at a location for intelligent life.

Despite our breakthrough, we still knew very little of the composition of dark matter. We figured out how to manipulate it, but like a child playing with a weapon, we had no idea how truly dangerous that was.

We had no idea dark matter was, in a way we cannot comprehend, alive.

I don't know why it took the planet instead of the ship. This is speculation, but I think when we changed dark matter, we HURT it, in a way that a carbon based animal cannot comprehend.

While orbiting, we got a distress signal from control. A giant, almost undetectable mass was surrounding Earth, and suddenly, any baryonic matter (matter made of atoms) began to change, shrinking in size. The distance between chemical bonds became smaller, until they merged into single atoms. All of humanity, and the planet, merged together into a plasma like mass, before dissipating, like a star would after dying.

We tried contacting control, but I don't think any of us expected a response.

Only two people remain in my crew. We were sitting down for another silent dinner when I decided to type this all up. The others lost hope much faster than us, but we're getting close to joining them soon.

I guess the Great Filter was right after all. I wonder how many other civilizations cracked the code of faster than light travel, only to be destroyed by the force they sought control over.

We can't leave. We can't travel fast enough to go anywhere, because the dark matter will wipe us out. We can't just pick a direction and fly away, because we don't have a reasonable destination to go to.

All we can do is land on the moon as it drifts out of orbit, regretting humanity's greatest discovery.

Bump in the Night

"You can't spell 'country' without 'cunt,'" James chuckled at his own joke.

"You're actually supposed to." I groaned, shuffling through CDs with him, trying to settle what to listen to next.

It had been three days since my building was quarantined, James had been over for a quick beer to catch up, and got stuck in my building. We didn't have cell service, but the government officials that sealed our building off got our work contact information and explained the situation.

Probably more than they did for us. Static burst through the television the night after the building was sealed up, waking us both up but only displaying one sentence;

"Has HE gone bump in the night yet?"

Luckily for the both of us, I had gotten groceries a few days before, so it's not like we would starve. I wondered how our neighbors were doing, whatever weird dome they used to seal the building shut most of the doors into individual apartments, so there was no efficient way to communicate. We'd hear thumps and yelling, but they never answered us shouting through the walls.

Honestly, James and I hadn't hung out in ages, and it was nice to catch up, but cabin fever was beginning to merge with the lack of information, and we were starting to get on each other's nerves.

Hence the music debate.

We had a few more beers, because why not? We aren't driving anywhere. I crawled into my bed, James curled up on the couch with a borrowed blanket, and we settled in for night number four.

Loud thuds woke us both up. I have a small pistol, so I grabbed that from under the bed while James ducked behind me. Another slam, this time coming from inside my bedroom closet.

We looked at each other. James gestured toward the door, I sighed, and slinked forward to yank the door open.

Inside was an emaciated, old man. He looked like a strange blend of people, I couldn't get a good grasp on his race, and his skin tone was unlike anything I've ever seen. He glanced at me with mismatched eyes, one blue and one green, and began sobbing.

James walked up to the man, but as soon as he put an arm on his shoulder, both of them began to scream. James' arm began to melt, the man roared laughter as he seemed to absorb James into himself, leaving a small pile of clothes on the ground. "You can't spell 'country' without 'cunt,'" The man-thing croaked.

It looked at me now, my hands gripping the pistol and shaking. Suddenly I began to recognize its appearance. The eyes belonged to my neighbors, one blue and one green, the hair belonged to my landlady, the voice to James.

I yelled for someone to help before realizing I was the last person in my building that hadn't been touched by this thing. It took a step forward.

"All I need now, is a heart." It growled.

Mass Snaps

Ever since the app came out, I've loved Snapchat. I send snaps of my daily life to all of my friends, and while I like the idea of the story feature, nothing beats getting a personal response from all my friends when I send them little jokes or stories from my life.

While this may sound pathetic, I started working third shift recently, which means I don't have a lot of time to see my friends, since I'm asleep while they're awake, or I'm awake and at work while they're asleep. Yeah, it's a dumb app, and the little 10 second pictures can't replace human interaction, but in my current position, it fills that void just enough to make me feel a little less alone.

I wake up Saturday morning (more like 6 in the afternoon, but "morning" doesn't mean much anymore) and the first thing I do is grab my phone to shut my alarm off. After I shower, brush my teeth, and finish all the other little rituals we do in the morning, I make a quick breakfast of eggs and toast. I take a snap of the eggs once they're made, and send a snap with the timestamp on it, aware how odd it will be for people to see I'm eating breakfast towards the evening. I chuckle to myself, knowing it's not funny or clever, not even a joke, really, but sending it all the same.

Almost instantly, I get a reply. My friend Henry, who never normally replies to snaps unless they're questions, already sent me a return snap. I'm a little confused, but open it anyway. Henry is sitting in his living room, a finger over his mouth, his eyes almost bugging out of his head. He looks exhausted and terrified, and as I noticed these details I started to read the thin line of text he sent with this picture.

"It's coming for you today."

Weird. I dismissed this easily, since Henry almost never snaps me anyway, and either meant to send this to somebody else, or was just playing a weird prank on me that I wasn't in on. I ate my breakfast, wondering what to do with my day (night) off. Since everybody in town is gone for the weekend, I settle on smoking a bowl of weed and playing video games by myself. Again.

I turn the lights on in my basement and light my bowl. As soon as I take my first inhale and cough, my phone buzzes. I open it to see a notification from my ex-girlfriend, Jessica. We parted on good terms, and still talked all the time. I smile a little, and open the snap. She sat in the same position as Henry, eyes bugged out a little, finger over her mouth, and the only difference in this snap was I recognized her bedroom walls. A line of text was there, and I looked down to read it.

"It's coming for you today."

At this point the first hit I took is kicking in, along with the paranoia it can bring. I switch to the phone app and call her, but she doesn't pick up. I hang up after I get the voicemail message, and snap her back. I look angry in the picture, and a little baked, but add in my line of text asking if she'd been talking to Henry.

After I get back to my room, I decide to look at my snap history, to see how many people have opened my snap from earlier. As I do, I notice I have several unopened snaps from my friends. My internet connection is shit, so my phone must have not registered the notifications. I open about ten snaps from friends, and each one fills me with more and more dread. All of them are the same, my friends using the front facing camera, a finger over the mouths, looking terrified with their eyes bugging out.

"It's coming for you today."
"It's coming for you today."
"It's coming for you today."

The sentence is burned into my mind, even as I close my eyes. The combination of the situation and the high is causing a headache, and I take a few deep breaths to try to calm down. I sit in silence for a little, before my phone buzzes again. I look and see a new member has added me on snapchat. I don't recognize the name, but the app says they added me by my own username. I see two friends have sent me snaps since this new person added me, but I ignore them and accept the invite.

I hear a knock on my door, but since it's late and everyone I know is out of town, I ignore it. I have more important things going on at the moment than a door to door salesman or lifeless Jehovah's Witness. I snap the new person, and ask what's happening. This is either some elaborate prank, or this is all connected. The new person sends a reply almost immediately. I hesitate, but open the snap. The screen is dark, but I can make out a faint outline of a person in it, finger against their lips. My eyes roll down to the line of text present, almost popping out itself among the dark background.

"It's here."

The message just registers in my head when I hear my front door shatter.

Meeting My Boyfriend's Parents for the First Time

Meeting your significant other's parents for the first time is a daunting ordeal. When Patrick said his parents wanted me over for dinner, I knew I'd have to do everything I could to make it a perfect evening.

His house was across town, but he offered to pick me up and drop me off after. I didn't want my mom asking me a million questions afterward, so I told her I was going to a friend's house to work on a group project.

He picked me up at 6, giving me a soft peck on the cheek as he put the car in reserve. He opened both the car door and his front door, holding them open like a perfect gentleman. He took my coat, wrapping it up unceremoniously in the closet.

"I got to run to the bathroom, I'll meet you in the living room after, okay?" He asked. "They're already waiting to meet you."

Before I could come up with an excuse, he cut me off.

"Don't worry, it'll give you a chance to get to know them as an individual, not just as the girl I brought over."

I conceded the point. Patrick grinned and jogged down the hall, and I walked the opposite way into the open living room.

I let out a chuckle when I saw Patrick sitting alone on the couch, his nose in a book. "Does the house loop around or something? Nice trick."

He gave me a confused look. "You're...Gina, right?" He sat up. "Patrick has told us a lot about you."

"You're his brother?" Patrick never mentioned he had siblings, let alone a twin. God, they looked just like each other, it was uncanny.

"Something like that." He held his grin longer than he should have. We sat in silence, he kept staring at me with that weird grin. After a few moments that felt like hours, I felt a little uncomfortable, so I excused myself to find the bathroom, hoping I'd run into Patrick on the way.

I opened the last door down the hall, assuming it was the bathroom, since it was where I saw Patrick heading last. Dark stairs greeted me, out of morbid curiosity, I descended them.

Tears welled up in my eyes and a scream died in my throat when I reached the bottom.

Countless girls were chained to the walls, some looked unconscious, and others looked dead. A few were rotten.

Most horrifying of all, some were pregnant.

"Help me…" a blonde haired girl said, her belly swollen and her eyes sunken.

I ran forward, pathetically trying to yank the chains out of the wall. I had to ask Patrick what was going on, why did his family have all these girls down here? "Who did this to you?" I asked the girl.

"The...the Patrick's did."

Huh? "What do you mean? His family?" I asked desperately, panic starting to set in.

"There is no family." She coughed, struggling to stay conscious. "They're all Patrick. We're just breeding stock for more of the-"

She cut herself off, shielding her face as the basement door opened.

Dozens of different boys, all looking like Patrick, walked down the stairs, identical sardonic dark grins on every one of their faces.

The door slammed shut.

The Best Medicine

Timmy heard a funny joke in class, and started laughing. He tried to tell his friends, but couldn't get through a sentence without laughing. It didn't matter, as soon as Timmy started talking, his friends started laughing, too.

The teacher tried to quiet them down, but when she found she couldn't keep herself from laughing long enough to quiet them now. It spread around the school the way a common cold would, and soon the police became involved.

Only one police officer escaped, the rest collapsed into a pile, laughing hysterically. The officer had put ear plugs in, kept his eyes closed, and spoke nothing. He thought he alone dodged whatever was going on, but a day later, woke up in the middle of the night, tears running down his face from laughter. Whatever was happening had been delayed, but not stopped.

It didn't take long to spread. Soon the whole town was laughing, to the point where neighboring cities heard it from a distance. When they went to investigate, they found the situation hilarious, they couldn't stop laughing at it.

Ireland was the first to fall, which makes sense since it started there. It was dubbed an epidemic of mass hysteria, and everyone was told to stay inside until the government could figure out how to stop, or at least slow, the spread.

It didn't work. Not only were there those that didn't listen, but those that stayed home heard the laughter on the news, or in the streets, and they too became infected. Soon broadcasts were shut down to prevent any more stories, but the damage was done. There wasn't one spot left on the planet that was silent, Earth was covered in laughing humans.

It took about a week. People began to die off. Exhaustion and thirst were the primary killers, starvation and accidental death followed. A large number of people were able to off themselves towards the end, when it became clear there was no cure or future. They tried swallowing pills, but couldn't relax their throats long enough to get them down, and had to resort to shooting themselves, laughing and smiling the whole time as they watched their friends and family die.

All of a sudden, the Earth was silent. Not deadly silent, there was still the sound of wind, birds, bugs; nature still went on, but not a single human soul was left on Earth.

Gaia crawled out of the ground, outside the school where this all started. She wasn't sure what else to do, she knew the humans would ruin the planet soon, but felt bad killing them, as they were part of nature. She infected Timmy first, she had seen the children laughing hard at recess earlier, and decided that would be a merciful way to go. In her mind, she gave humans a peaceful death, she allowed them to pass in a state that she learned to be associated with euphoria.

Gaia inhaled a breath of dirty air, motivated by the idea that soon the air and water would taste as pure as they used to, in the days before the apes began living in tribes.

Knowing her plan had worked, and the Earth was saved, Gaia began to laugh.

Mr. Sticky

My name is Sabrina, I am 17 years old, and I have a big problem lurking toward me.

Mr. Sticky. That's what I called him, anyway.

It was strange, the older I got, the more he seemed to be a part of my upbringing. I remembered him being there playing in the sandbox with me, encouraging me at the dentist's office, and even sitting with my parents for a few Christmas mornings. He was a tall man with a top hat and too many arms, a face that looked like it had been partially drawn and left for later, and piercing yellow eyes.

When I asked them, Mom and Dad told me he must've been an imaginary friend, because the name "Mr. Sticky" meant nothing to them. They didn't know who he was, and were concerned if an adult they didn't know had been talking to me without them around. I assured them that Mr. Sticky must have just been a figment of my imagination after all.

Oh, but that felt like a lie.

It wasn't until I was in high school that I figured it out. The older I got, and the more of my past that I stopped remembering, got replaced by time with Mr. Sticky. I remembered him being there, on the first day of high school, even though there's a picture my mom took of me walking into the building alone.

It's not just that he's imaginary, he's a retroactive imaginary friend. When I forget little things, like the old house my parents lived in before we moved, it gets replaced with something involving Mr. Sticky.

I no longer remember the layout of my parents' old house, but I could draw you the blueprints to our town's sewer system. I remember Mr. Sticky showing me how to navigate them, though I don't think I've ever been down there.

Also, the older I get, the angrier he seems. I remember him being friendly, almost playful, but as I got older he got scarier and scarier. I remember him at my 13th birthday party, growling at me from inside some bushes. I remember him at my aunt's funeral, laughing and licking the coffin. I remember him crawling on the ceiling of our cabin when we went up north.

I remember him last month, screaming at me and trying to chase me into the sewers.

He's getting closer, I can feel it. Most of my childhood is a blur, and despite my parents having photographs proving otherwise, I hardly remember growing up with them. All I remember from my childhood is the dark tunnels and sharp odor of the sewers. Mom says I've never been down there, but I remember falling asleep on a pile of garbage....

Last week is the reason I'm writing this. I remember waking up to Mr. Sticky sitting in my bedroom, watching me sleep. I asked him what he wanted, but he just laughed and muttered "soon".

I'm not sure what to do. Eventually Mr. Sticky is going to catch up to my memories. I'm not sure if he exists within me or because of me. I think he's trapped in there somehow, infecting my memories because he has nowhere else to live.

The longer it takes him to escape, the angrier he gets. I've known him my whole life. My parents insist I was only eight when I first asked them about Mr. Sticky, but I have memories of him predating my eighth birthday.

He's starting infecting memories from just days ago. I don't know how much longer I have until he catches up, what will happen to me if he does, or even what he wants.

If anyone else starts remembering a man that doesn't exist, try to get help faster than I did.
Because as far as I can think, I am out of options.

It's Too Late

Every night before I fall asleep, I think of all the things I could be doing differently with my life.

Some nights I think about how I could go back to school, get a degree in something I actually enjoy, instead of just wage slaving away at my nine to five, waiting for a quick two day weekend.

Some nights I think about going out and meeting a nice girl. Maybe even downloading one of those stupid dating apps. Getting married would be nice, having a son or daughter to watch grow up, guiding them in the right direction.

Some nights I think about travel. How I could go anywhere I wanted, just cut loose and start a new life. Just get on a train and let the ride wash my old name away whenever I get tired of being someone new.

Some nights I wonder what it'd be like to finish my novel. I have three folders of random information, plot lines, even character drawings, but no concrete pages written. Even if I couldn't get it published, I could at least be proud that I accomplished something.

Some nights I think about learning a new instrument. I used to play piano, not very well, but I always wanted to be able to pick up a guitar and sing one of my favorite songs. Not in front of a crowd, just around a fire with some friends.

Some nights I dream about living a simple life, working on a farm somewhere out in the country. Waking up and falling asleep with the sun, being in sync with all the animals and crops in my care.

The possibilities are endless.

Well, they were.

Tonight, though, I think about where I'm at. Some run down nursing home, being taken care of by underpaid nursing aides who would rather be anywhere else besides their place of employment. Just like me eighty years ago.

Some nights I think of all the things I could have done differently with my life.

But now it's too late for me.

Don't let it be too late for you.

I Used To Bully a Kid in Middle School

I called him every word you can think of. The F-word, the N-word, the C-word, the Z-word (don't ask).

It got to the point where nobody wanted to be friends with him, for fear of association. It made him a social outcast, and I became the king of 7th grade. He was a smart kid, gifted even; that only made it easier for me. If I remember right, he skipped a grade or two because of how fast he could process information. He was a genius, but for all that intellect, he could never figure out to act like a normal kid. He'd melt dolls on the playground at recess, hiss at people when they tried to touch him, make up weird stories about how he'd go monster hunting on weekends like a hero.

Back when you're 13, you made stupid choices and do stupid things, mostly because you don't understand that all of you have the rest of your lives left. You don't understand that your classmates, even if they are weird or annoying, are also individual people, and deserve to be treated as such.

The regret didn't kick in for me until senior year of high school. I had heard that the kid was released from a psych ward after some mental breakdown, and felt that I might be partially to blame. Rumor had it he was on serious meds, but was taking classes from home.

He had taken a turn when he got to high school, and the class size increased. Instead of branching out and meeting new people, he became even more secluded, surrounded by people he felt would never understand him. I didn't see him much in those four years, but felt that my constant teasing and taunts had convinced him he'd always be different.

I wanted to call him and apologize for being such an asshole, I wanted to send him a hand written letter explaining that I was a stupid kid, I wanted to get coffee with him and tell me that I should have been better.

That's the thing about apologizing when you know you're wrong; it's painful.

I turned out to be a burnout, in the end. My college grades slipped as my blood alcohol levels rose, and soon enough I got a letter of expulsion.

I was grateful to get a fast food job after a few years of drifting, even though I was humiliated. Being 26 years old and having a rude teenager for a boss is a sickening feeling, something I wouldn't wish on anyone.

The job was easy enough though. To the point where I'd start sneaking my flask during bathroom breaks, or having a quick beer in my car while on break.

I'm not proud of it, but you can only get the manager for so many Karen's before you mentally slip a little. Cleaning up shit outside the toilet (Seriously? How and why do people do that?), making trash food in a deep fryer while covered in sweat, and having people complain if you miss a small detail in their meal will whittle away at anyone. I'd love to see politicians work a minimum wage job like that, they'd break down in minutes, vote to raise wages all around, I bet.

That night, the accident was my fault. My flask had been emptied after a hard day, and I didn't stop at the red light. Nobody died, but I put myself and a family in the hospital. The two children were admitted to the ICU, the mother released but stood vigil over his sons. The father was in a coma, they were unsure how badly his brain was damaged, when or if he'd ever wake up.

I needed emergency surgery. I know that because the anesthesia didn't take. I was wide awake, wired even. I managed to glance over at the surgeon, hoping to get his attention somehow, hopeful as he met my eyes with a warm smile. Sterilization liquids and hand sanitizer scents filled the surgical room, two nervous aides were present, following the surgeon like scared little deer. I wanted to groan that I was being used as an example, but what anesthesia was working prevented me from making any noise.

He rattled off the exact procedures he'd be doing to me, promising the aides I was out cold, even though my eyes were open. He said it was a thing some trauma patients did, as their bodies went into overdrive to keep them alive. Something about the brain trying to catch up with what's happening to the body. The aides must've been cheating in their classes, because they accepted this explanation with no questions at all.

He told them not to be nervous, as he had overcome lots of personal obstacles to get to his position, and the aides would most likely do the same.

I couldn't move when it clicked why his voice sounded so familiar, but I wanted to squirm and shake, anything to get their attention so they'd postpone the surgery.

I felt the knife slice my chest open, felt the pull of skin across my ribs, felt the pressure of my punctured lung deflate, felt the CRACK as my broken sternum was rearranged, felt the setting of broken ribs. I felt all of it, every little slice or scratch or tear.
I even felt his hot breath in my ear when the aides weren't looking.

"Remember me?" He grinned manically, laughing under his breath.

Turns out, there are far more painful things than just apologizing.

#

Do you know how starfish eat?

They extend their stomach out through their mouth, spilling digestive enzymes over their food, partially digesting prey outside their body before consuming it.

I'm telling you this, because the creatures that came to Earth do the same thing before they eat us.

I will brag a little bit, and say we humans lasted longer than we should have. The creatures were much taller and stronger than us, faces resembling a gargoyle, body covered in eyes and giant mouths. Bullets didn't do much to them, and even if you managed to hack one up, they'd regenerate, each part becoming a full, adult creature within a day.

Reports indicated that the digestive process was, well, painful. Even during consumption, after being pumped full of acid and a slurry of enzymes, people would still be alive to feel multiple mouths bite into them. Their teeth were soft, hence the outside digestion mechanism, but this meant consuming prey would take much longer than was merciful.

Most of the human race had died in horrified agony. My wife had killed herself months ago, guilty after our younger daughter was eaten by one of those... things, after I had seduced her during her watch duty. I'm sitting alone in an abandoned basement with my son, reading him an old book we found inside this person's house. I always wanted to be a good parent, and for eight years I got to think I was. I was selfish as a teenager, and had never quite grown out of that. Now the best I can do is distract my little boy from the constant screams and slurping sounds that seemed to follow us no matter where we go.

I hold my pistol in my hands. I have to do it tonight. I have only one bullet left, and I don't want my son to go like my daughter did. I'm preparing to do it, I want him to feel somewhat safe and fall asleep first, knowing he is loved.

I never want him to know I'm the one doing this to him.

Suddenly there's banging and crashes coming from upstairs. My son screams, giving us away, and I hear repeated slamming on the basement door.

My son looks at me, probably hoping for a plan, but I have nothing to offer him. I think about how awful the screams are as people are slowly torn apart like wet bread, or the hissing as the acid is injected into their pores, the high pitch in their pleas for mercy or even just a faster death.

There's a few creatures rushing down the stairs, it's always worse in packs. They tear you up limb by limb and split you evenly amongst themselves.

Nobody should have to die like that.

I always wanted to be a good parent.

But I was always so damn selfish.

"I'm sorry." I guiltily tell my son, before holding the pistol under my chin, screaming before I pull the trigger.

Whites Only

The sign was displayed next to a confederate flag, a mark of pride for the owner's heritage and obedience to the ways of Jim Crow. It forbade her entry, and right now, that was the only thing she wanted.

"Sir, please-" She began desperately. "I just need a bottle of water, I'll pay you double; if I have to walk across town to another store I'll pass out."

Ruby wasn't lying or exaggerating. It was over a hundred degrees out, the fact that Ruby had made it to the store closest to her apartment was a miracle. Walking across town on her old, tired legs might very well be the end of her.

The owner grinned through tobacco stained teeth, holding a shotgun he grabbed from under the counter. "I'll blow you's away if you's even try to enter, don't you's kind know how to read?" He pointed his weapon at the sign.

"I'll pay double, triple, please." Her lips were chapped and dry. A simple request, a bottle of water, for three times the value.

For a few seconds she got her hopes up, seeing the owner grab a small water bottle, placing it right beside the entrance.

"If you's can get it without coming inside, it's all yours." He smirked, spitting a brown blob of dip from his mouth. "But if you's step even one toe in here, I'll blow you away, n-"

She didn't hear the rest of the sentence, but she didn't have to. There was not going to be any appeal to reason, any mercy, any rational dialogue spoken here.

She sighed, and turned around. A group of five white men were heading towards the store. "Ma'am," the tallest one said, looking down at Ruby, and tipped his hat.

Ruby turned around, mostly just to see the store owners face. Naturally, he looked revolted, as if he had just watched the world flip upside down. In a way he had, Ruby doubted he'd ever seen another white man act even a little courteous to a colored woman before.

She watched the men go inside, before one violently yanked the shotgun out of the owner's hands. The other four pulled pistols out of their pockets while the tallest man began shouting.

A robbery. Perfect, if she didn't die of thirst, she might be framed, even lynched for stealing.

"Help me! Run in here and do something!" He begged Ruby desperately.

She did. Ruby honestly almost did, despite having no weapons or chance of fighting this group of men. But stopped herself when she read the sign again.

"I'm not allowed."

The tallest man looked back at Ruby, smiling. After she gestured to the water, he tossed it to her, tipping his hat once again before aiming his firearm at the owner.

The world was harsh and cruel to Ruby and her family, but today was a sliver of vengeance, a small strike back.
She turned to go home, savoring the water while reveling in the sound of screams and gunfire, smiling and humming to herself all the way.

Rough and Steep

The hill is wet, not quite frozen but cold enough to be perilously slippery.

I've been climbing for a week. The way up to the top is rough and steep, but beautiful fields lie just beyond the top. The view of a lifetime. I just have to survive the climb.

Switchbacks stopped occurring a few miles ago; the mountain got so steep that even added them would have defeated the purpose. I've been walking, stumbling, camping, and sleeping in incline for days now.

It's so hard. My legs are so sore, blisters cover my feet, my head is constantly pounding, but I know I can't stop climbing. If I stop, I might lose the will to go on, I might consider those beautiful fields not worth the trip, I might not want to put in the work that precedes the good things in life.

And so I keep climbing. I've slipped and tumbled a few times now, no broken bones yet, although my nose is busted up. Blood fills my boots, from the constant rubbing of blisters. Water has been low for days, I've been boiling ice that I scrounge around.

I'm not sure why I'm still climbing. I know it's only been about a week but it feels closer to a month. I haven't seen another hiker in days, they all must have considered this path too dangerous this time of year. I wanted an adventure, but now I'm not so sure.

I've started seeing things, too. Formless shapes in the distance, yelling at me to wake up when I lie down to rest, telling me I have to keep going.

Despite the encouragement, they terrify me. They all sound familiar, but I can't place them. I feel I've seen their faces also, but I can't make them out, like they've been censored on a television or something. I'm afraid if I stop, the things will catch up to me.

And so I keep climbing. Despite how tired I am; despite how much I hurt and ache.

I need to see what happens when I get to the top.

"How long has he been out, doctor?" Priscilla asked, worry filling her face.

"A few days. He had a rough fall from the mountain, he should never have been out climbing this late in the season." The doctor said, in a tone that was both pitiful and scornful. "He has differing levels of action. Sometimes his blood pressure and pulse speed up, sometimes they slow down. It's like he still thinks he's hiking."

Priscilla stared at her father's battered body, tubes coming out all around him to keep him functioning, and began to cry. She wondered what her father was going through; what it'd be like to be comatose, unaware of the world around you, but still physically alive.

She worried he was in pain or scared, but the doctor dismissed her fears. Even he didn't know what comatose people think about, if they think at all.

Spaghettification

Sounds like a made up term, but let me tell you, it's very real.

Basically, it's the concept of how objects get pulled into an event horizon inside the heart of a black hole.

Like most things, it sounds funny until it's you.

Our mission was to collect data around the black hole, but I got greedy. I wanted to collect as much data as possible; proving that Hawking radiation could be used as an energy source would cement my place as a giant in the scientific community.

No matter how much you cram a person's brain with math and physics knowledge, sometimes ambition takes ahold. I got too close, and got sucked into the black hole.

Most people assume the spaghettification process is just instant death. I mean, the body is stretched out to an unimaginable capacity, it shouldn't support biological function.

That would be true, if not for the time dilations.

Time and gravity and related, and the stage I am currently in is immeasurably short, and long.

Let me explain.

In the last zeptosecond (trillionth of a billionth of a second) before I died, time distorted around me in such a way where the spaghettification process will go on for what feels like an eternity. I've stopped trying to keep track of time, I'm in the middle of space being sucked into a void; time doesn't mean shit anymore.

And yes, before you ask, it's incredibly painful. Every muscle, bone, cell I have on my body is being dragged into an event horizon.

Since I'm already outside space-time, by definition, the normal rules don't apply. Which is why I'm still being dragged in extreme agony.

Here's the thing though, I can ignore that if I focus.

I can move through time as much as I want. I can go back to when I was a kid and relive my 12th birthday, when I lost my virginity after prom, when I got married and enjoy the day all over again.

I can't change anything, but I can relive it. Over and over again.

In the background of all of it, is pain. Even when I'm riding a snowmobile with my college friends, the back of my mind is receiving pain signals, reminding me of my inevitable fate.

Like I said, time doesn't mean much. I can go back and enjoy any moment I've lived, even observe things from an outside perspective. I've traveled to watch construction of the great wall, the first plane ride, even the founding of the states.

Again, I can't change anything, just observe. Kind of a shame I'll never be able to do anything with the knowledge.

One zeptosecond, stretched out forever.

I have no time to change my fate, yet all the time in the universe to consider it.

I don't think I'll survive passing the event horizon.

But if this is what it's like just being near it, I really want to know what I'll experience if I pass through.

Extended Warranty

I get two to three spam calls a day about my car's nonexistent extended warrant, and I'm sick of it.

Most of the time, I'm at work, so I simply silence my phone or deny the calls. As a millennial, I hate answering the phone, at all, but on my days off I absolutely LOVE getting these spam calls, because I can mess with the caller.

"Has this ever worked? On anyone?" I ask sometimes.

"I only own a horse and buggy, can't afford a car. Can you still sell me a warranty?" Stories I make up on the spot, always the most fun.

"So when you visit family on holidays, what do you tell them you do?" Every now and then they turn into personal insults, especially when they call when I'm still in bed and still grumpy.

Sometimes I just hold my throat and screech until they hang up. That's also pretty fun.

Spite motivates me here. I will wait on hold for fifteen minutes just for the chance to fuck with these people, and I don't feel bad. Their job is literally to scam normal, hardworking people out of money, I don't have any moral qualms about giving them a hard time if that's how they choose to make a living.

I got a call on the way to work from them, "Spam Risk" showing up on my caller ID. I accepted the call, listening to the hold music through my Bluetooth.

Finally I got to a person. "Hi, this is Ben from Car-Go! Can I get your vehicle year and model?" The loser asked, his voice nasally and weak.

"Yeah, I've got a nicer car than you do, because I have skills and work for a living. You've probably got a rental that you rent on odd weekdays to get back and forth to your scam artist job." I spat out, annoyed at both the call and the string of red lights I've been hitting.

"Do you think yourself funny, Matthew?" His voice asked, ice cold. "I was laid off and forced into this job, how would you feel if you were just as helpless?"

I groaned. The sympathy card was new, but not unexpected. "You're scamming people to help yourself. You're a parasite, and you make me sick."

He chucked, so unlike the whiny kid that had answered. "I'll be seeing you very soon, Matthew. Unless you want to give me your information here and now."

I refused, swore at him a little more, and then hung up. It left me unnerved all day. My phone kept buzzing from spam numbers, to the point where I had to put in on airplane mode just to avoid the annoyance.

After work, I slumped into my car, exhausted. I start it up, letting it run for a little before putting it in gear, waiting for the windshield to defrost so I can actually see the road in front of me. I feel a little sting at my neck, startled that a bug got in my car; it's December, after all.

Suddenly my hands slump down, and I found I couldn't move my body. My phone began to buzz, and a voice in the back seat spoke up.

"This is Ben from Car-Go! We've been trying to reach you about your car's extended warranty."

Forbidden Love

Call it science, or magic, or voodoo, I don't really care.

I had personally figured out how to bring someone back from the dead.

I knew this could help everyone on Earth, but my research was selfish in nature.

You see, I wanted to see my lover one last time.

Almost everyone disapproved of our love. I think it was the age difference. They called me a cougar, joked I was a pedophile, some claimed I was a monster. But we didn't care, he always would tell me he loved me after we made love.

Our connection was so strong. We knew each other so well, but we had to move around a lot, wherever we went people didn't seem tolerant of our love.

As wonderful and beautiful as our love was, it was forbidden. But all we had was each other.

I blame all of THEM. The ones who couldn't understand. The ones who sneered in disgust, whispering to their ailing and aging husbands about who I choose to love. I've always been a "my body, my choice" kind of gal, so I never let them get to me.

But they got to him. I found him in our bedroom with an empty bottle of pills and a note, professing hatred of the world and his regret of passing.

I stand over his casket now, caked in mud and grime. I worked the process, pressing my ear against the coffin, squealing like a school girl with delight when I heard panicked breathing.

I need him back. He was my rock, my world, the feeling of him inside me was too much to lust for, and nothing would satisfy me except him.

I lifted the lid, grasping him tight. He groaned, and began sobbing. "Please. No. No, no more."

"Hush darling. It's going to be okay. Mommy's here." I sweetly whisper into my son's ears, while he sobs with joy in the empty graveyard.

#

Prions are misfolded proteins with the ability to transmit their misfolded shape onto normal variants of the same protein.

Basically, a glitch in biological life. There's no cure, it can take years for symptoms to develop, and by the time you notice it, your neurological systems are already fucked beyond repair.

People celebrated when the asteroid broke up in space. Parts of it scattered into dust in our atmosphere, softly pattering the Earth in a thin, dark snow.

We wouldn't have celebrated if we knew what the asteroid was composed of.

Scientists collected the biggest samples they could find, and in a panic they informed the public that the asteroid was primarily composed of misfolded biological proteins, and they had potentially infected the planet's upper atmosphere.

Anarchy followed, every time someone felt a tickle in their throat or a pounding headache, they assumed it was the prion disease catching up with them, and they rushed to their doctor for answers.

It took years for any real symptoms to appear, but by then society had panicked themselves into near collapse. People assumed they all had a finite amount of time left to be themselves, and those people were correct.

The first person to manifest symptoms was a little girl with an already compromised immune system in South Africa. She claimed her skin 'burned' and began to take on a dark blue hue. Her hair fell out, and her bones increased in size and density, matching the structure of an adult male.

Before the process was complete, other people began displaying the same symptoms. The prion changed people, misfolding and altering the tertiary structure of their proteins to match an unknown original organism, a blue, male extraterrestrial humanoid with bronchial tubes jutting out their backs, expelling more prions into the air around them.

All of the 'Changed' as they became known had an innate desire to return home, though they could not explain where or what that was. The Changed no longer required sleep, not comprehending the action at all, and devoted a large amount of time to developing space travel, hoping to leave Earth behind.

The Changed were not aggressive, and wouldn't seek out humans to infect, insisting that nature would take its course by itself.

Of course, they were right, 99% of humanity had been infected with the initial asteroid, so time was the only variable.

Humans spent decades looking for extraterrestrial life, never expecting to find it in the form of a broken protein.

Humanity had been altered forever, finally ready to journey out past the stars and discover new worlds.

All it took was the complete and final annihilation of the properties that made them human in the first place.

White Eyed Woman

The average time for an ambulance to arrive on the scene in Oshkosh is about 11 minutes.

I mention this, because walking home at night can be scary for women, especially those like me with a wild imagination. As a 4th year college student, (and being a 5'3" woman) I had somewhat gotten used to the feeling of walking alone in the dark, but still tried to avoid it as much as possible. That weekend, my best friend Brian and I had gone to the bars to relieve some midterm stress. Brian was a nice guy, but I only saw him as a best friend, nothing more. We both got teased over this, but neither of us seemed to take it to heart, and we always got along great.

And then he saw the white eyed woman.

You may have heard of her before. The only reason I have is because Brian saw her years ago, when he almost died. We were walking home from the bars of Oshkosh late one Saturday night, and a mugger jumped out at us. He pulled out a bowie knife, and demanded we give him our money.

"You can have my purse, but please let me get my keys out first." I begged, reaching into my purse to yank them out. Bad move.

He must've thought I was reaching for my phone or a gun, and he raced forward with his knife, about to slash down at my chest.

I always wondered if Brian had actual feelings for me, and I felt my suspicion was confirmed when he threw himself between me and the knife. Crimson blood pooled out of his arm where the slash had appeared, the serrated part of the knife tearing through flesh, and the mugger jumped back, looking almost as surprised as I did. The knife fell to the sidewalk, as the man screamed and ran. His evening didn't seem to be going to plan.

Unfortunate for him. More unfortunate for us.

I ran to Brian as he fell, his left arm slashed open. I could tell it was bad because he took one look at it and turned pale. Brian was a pre-med student, and I could tell by his face he was going to have to shift into survival mode. The cut went vertically down his arm, the way one would slash their wrist properly to commit suicide. Brian looked up at me, pointed to my sweatshirt, and said in a barely audible whisper; "Tourniquet."

It was like something shifted for me. I pulled off my sweatshirt, yanked the hoodie string out of it, and began to wrap it right above his elbow to cut off blood flow. I only knew where to tie it off right away due to my enrollment as a 4th year nursing student. Brian was pre-med and a glorified Eagle Scout. In hindsight, both of us may have been the best equipped duo on campus for this situation, although it felt so alien to us at the time. The panic that set in earlier was slowly ebbing back in, I began to fumble my knots, almost bursting into tears two (or ten) times. Once I was confident the makeshift tourniquet was set, I pulled out my phone and dialed 911, my fingers leaving bloody prints on the screen. I didn't care, and pressed the phone to my ear.

I must've sounded terrible on the phone because the operator told me to calm down at least three times. The situation was explained, and both an emergency vehicle and the police were on their way. With nothing else to do but wait, I sat down next to Brian and cradled his head in my lap.

"You almost died for me." I muttered. More for me than him. I did feel terrible, and now was either the worst or perfect time to discuss this. He smiled at me, muttered something about that being what friends do, but then jerked his head away from me suddenly.

"Who is that?" He muttered weakly. I followed his eyes and saw nobody. It was too late for any bar stragglers to be walking home, and I was focused on making sure he stayed conscious until the paramedics got there. I looked at his face, and instead of the reassuring smile he had a second ago, there was only terror. "There's no one here," I told him, trying to keep him calm. He was going to lose the arm, an unfortunate side effect of the tourniquet, but if he was hallucinating from blood loss, things were worse than I thought.

"The woman over there. She's staring at me." I looked again, and saw...nobody. This was bad. I tried to hold back tears, but I felt some trickle down my face anyway. I glanced back down at my friend, and saw he was no longer awake. I slapped him in the face and screamed. He gasped and looked back at the sidewalk. I'll never forget the look on his face. I've never seen anyone in the world look that scared in my life.

"She's closer." He gasped. I had to look for a third time, and it confirmed my fears, nobody was standing there. I would have been less concerned if there was a woman walking towards us. I tried telling Brian this, but he began to panic, which would have been funny is the situation wasn't so fucked up. I heard sirens in the distance, and my spirits lifted.

He was going to be fine. Damaged, yet alive. But he wouldn't stop staring at the sidewalk.

Finally, I tried to maintain a conversation, both to keep him focused on staying conscious and to calm him down. But I'd only a word in before he'd look up at me pleadingly.

"Beth, please don't let her come near me, I don't like her." I asked what he meant, but he shook his head. "Her eyes are all white, she keeps getting closer but she never moves. She's grinning at me now, fuck, I think she can hear me, fuck!"

I knew I shouldn't encourage this delusion, but I wanted him to stay awake, so I asked more questions. Brian didn't give me too many details, besides the woman having black hair, white eyes, and a red dress. Between all these details, he seemed to pass out for a second or two, before realizing where he was again. Finally, he pulled my head down by the hair. I yelled in pain, but he pulled my ear next to his mouth, and whispered "She's right behind you, and she won't stop grinning at me."

I'll admit it, I burst into tears as the ambulance arrived a minute later.

Not wanting to leave his side, let alone go home, I spent the night on a bench outside the E.R. I got some weird looks, before I realized I was wearing clothes covered in damp blood. I called a friend to bring me some new clothes from my apartment, as well as toiletries, like my toothbrush and some tampons (because OF COURSE I'd start my cycle at that moment). The doctor woke me up a few hours later.

My fears were right, they had to amputate his arm. But the doctor reassured me it was the best case scenario, we did the best we could, we were very brave, etcetera. He gave me permission to see Brian, and I almost ran into his hospital room.

His family was still on their way, being from Minnesota, and his other friends were probably just waking up to read my hundred texts explaining the situation. I was surprised to find him awake. He must've needed to rest badly, but somehow he was alert and smiling at me as I burst into his room, slamming the door against the wall.

We made small talk at first, mostly because I wanted to see how alert and aware he really was. He made a few jokes about how he needed to find a girlfriend now, since his left was his 'you know what' arm. I burst out laughing at that one. After all this, the guy was making jokes. He was a little scared of the morphine they pumped into him, but it seemed to relax him a lot more once it kicked in.

I couldn't help but ask about the woman, and I instantly regretted asking, because he tried to pull himself out of bed, falling back on the mattress since he no longer had a left forearm to lean on. He began to panic, asking me where and who the woman was. I tried to calm him down, but eventually the nurse had to sedate him.

I felt so much worse after that.

I stayed at the hospital for two whole days. Friends brought me food and lecture notes, and the professors knew either Brian or I would miss their lectures unless there was an emergency, and even came to visit him. Brian's biochem professor joked that I must love him very much to stay here this late. I stuck my tongue out at him while he laughed, but realized maybe he wasn't completely wrong.

The one good thing that came out of this fucked up situation was the staff at the hospital recognized the situation, and since I was almost out of school anyway, offered me a position at their hospital in the E.R. While a good job, it wasn't my dream, but I accepted it nonetheless. They even agreed to help me pay off my loans if I started there soon, so I had to agree. Brian's recovery was going great, partly because of his good nature and positive attitude, and I kissed him on the cheek before leaving the hospital for the first time in days.

Neither of us mentioned the woman for years.

After he finished med school, Brian applied to become a resident at the same hospital. They remembered him, not only because of his personality, but because they didn't need to amputate a lot of limbs there, so he had quite the college story. Most of his work was speaking to patients and doing simple tests, since he couldn't do surgery or E.R work with one arm. But he was happy, and soon enough we were together-but-not-really.

Six months after our friends with benefits situation turned into a relationship, I crashed my car driving home from a particularly long shift. The car rolled off the road, and I sat upside down in my seat, suspended by the seat belt. I dazed in and out of consciousness, trying to reach my phone, which was buried at the bottom of my purse. I called 911, tried my best to explain, and they sent people to help me. My arm was definitely broken, and my leg didn't feel so great either, but I felt fine.

Then I saw her too.

I understand why Brian had been so afraid. She looked like a normal woman, just staring at the car wreck, but her eyes were all white, and looked like they were rolled up in the back of her head. She wasn't moving, but her red dress was waving in the wind. I closed my eyes, thinking I was just remembering what Brian told me, but when I opened them, she was about a foot closer to the car.

She was grinning, looking like her face would split in half at any second.

The average time for an ambulance to arrive on the scene in Oshkosh is about 11 minutes.

I just hope the ambulance gets here faster than that. I don't know if I can stay awake long enough to keep her away.

Hypnic Jerk

It's happened to all of us at one. You're about to fall asleep, either for a quick nap, a long rest, or just nodding off in class. Then your brain decides to convince your body that you're falling, you race up, full of adrenaline, and find yourself safe and sound, your body seeming like it's just toying with you.

It's annoying as shit. I spent my time in grad school studying sleep medicine, and became fascinated with the topic. I even attended a lecture devoted to the phenomenon.

The explanation of it is simple, your body's muscles contract suddenly, as if in a panic. There's a few explanations, variables that fit different people depending on their habits; caffeine, dreams, anxiety, and for the most part, its person dependent why the hypnic jerk occurs.

There's another phenomenon that happens to people when they sleep that fascinated me; sleep paralysis. Your mind wakes up, but your body does not, and you sometimes undergo hallucinations. The body doesn't move as a defensive mechanism, you wouldn't want to physically act out your dreams all the time, right?

Before modern science, people chalked a lot of illness or phenomenon up to paranormal activity; alien abduction, ghosts, curses.

Demonic possession.

70% of people experience the hypnic jerk, and 40% of people experience sleep paralysis.

It's the 30% of people who don't have hypnic jerks that are the ones at risk.

I wrote my thesis on this, but I'm not sure I can turn it in. I'm not sure I can defend it with a straight face. That's why I'm putting this here, where other people can weigh in and offer advice.

Sleep paralysis isn't always a hallucination. Sometimes, it's caused by spirits called fairies. Simply put, they are disembodied spirits, leftovers from an age of demons and Gods, who have spent millennia searching for a new body.

They can only control a body that offers no resistance, but is still aware of its surroundings. This is where the legends of Changelings come from, people that got taken over by a fairy when they were sleeping. They mimic the person they control, but it's not perfect, and they sometimes get caught.

The body offers some resistance, however. When the fairy tries to enter a person, all the muscles will contract, and the spirit will be repelled. The hypnic jerk, a nuisance to be sure, but arguably one of the body's best defensive mechanisms.

Around 30% of people claim to not have experienced a hypnic jerk, and an even smaller percentage are physically unable to undergo one.

If a person in that small group undergoes sleep paralysis, without being able to undergo a hypnic jerk, they risk being taken over by a fairy, if one visits them during an episode. They'll wake up as someone completely new, trying to act the way they did before they were taken over. I'm working on different ways to spot people that aren't what they say they are, but I don't have a large sample size to work with. If you know anyone that started acting strangely out of nowhere, please let me know, they might be just what I'm looking for.

The next time you wake up startled, as if you were falling, don't get annoyed.

Just be glad you woke up at all.

The Glowing Lake

There's something wonderful to be said about the stillness of a lake when there's only one boat on it. It feels as though the rest of the world has been put on mute, and one can do or think about anything they want. Hundreds of fish can swim under the water, and birds can chirp as loud as they'd like, but it doesn't change the feeling of tranquility that comes with a boat paddling, making the only visible ripples in the water. Max hadn't been on the water for a few days, and was dying to get out there. He woke up before the rest of the world, poured himself some coffee, and was paddling out to the center of the lake by six.

Since retiring from his job as a translator, he had lots of days like this, where he could get out on the lake and be alone with his thoughts. But it was July, and all the tourists were all over the waters, being loud, partying, and leaving trash in the water. *They're going home soon*, he reminded himself, *and soon you can have your quiet mornings alone with the water again, whenever you want.*

Max was having those thoughts of peace when his oar hit a body. Being in the middle of the water, he turned to see what the obstruction was, and nearly screamed when he saw the corpse, facing down. Even though he knew the lake was empty, he looked around for help. Seeing nobody, he looked down at the body again, calming himself down as best he could, taking in more details to report to the police when he returned.

The man who Max had run into couldn't have been older than thirty. His skin was white but a little sunburnt, he was wearing a neon green shirt a similar color to the vest Max was wearing, camouflage athletic shorts, and a strap on his upper bicep that could fit an iPod (*he was running he was running and somebody must have killed him did they toss him in the lake to hide the body did he kill himself near the water and fall in did he drown?*)

Dozens of theories and ideas ran through Max's head, and by the time he snapped out of it enough to look for any marks on the body, he saw that the body was gone.

What the fuck? Did he sink? No, Max thought, *that couldn't be it*. Although he didn't get a good look at the face, he knew the body was still fresh. The skin hadn't started to rot, and the body had floated back to the surface after Max had hit it with his oar. It still had enough air left in it to float

Max started to look around him again, looking for any sign of the body, any bubbles or ripples indicating where it had moved. Across the lake, the sun was reflecting brightly off the lake. (*that's not the sun I can see so deep in the water that light can't be coming from above the water*)

Before he even had time to register the idea as crazy, Max knew he was right. *The lake is glowing. There's a light at the bottom of the lake, and it's fucking glowing.*

He had time to regret not bringing his cell phone to the lake before he heard the scratching. He kept looking, trying to find the source of the noise, before he realized it was coming from the boat. He checked the bottom, but didn't see anything by his feet moving around. It was a horrible, uneasy noise, like claws raking across a chalkboard. Max couldn't find the reason for the sound, unless...

(*it's coming under the fucking boat.*)

(*no, it can't be, that doesn't make sense.*)

(*the lake is glowing and a body disappeared, none of this makes sense.*)

While Max had a mental argument with himself, the scratching grew louder, and more aggressive, as if whatever was causing it was trying to dig its way through the surface. Finally, as Max was about to grab an oar and start racing back to his dock, it stopped.

He had time for a quick breath before he saw the white hands reach up on the side of the boat. He fell in surprise and fear, landing on his back and hitting his head on a seat. When he looked up again, he saw the body again, climbing up onto his boat.

It was obviously dead, but if one judged it with just a quick glance, they wouldn't have been able to tell. The body showed no signs of injury or struggle, not even a bruise or a small cut, but when it opened its eyes, they were pure white, and the pupils weren't visible or were gone. It opened its mouth, and an inhuman growl escaped its lips. Its arms and legs moved in a grotesque, broken sort of way, as if they had been frozen and were being used for the first time in a while.

But it has moved recently, it swam under the boat, Max thought frantically. *You rowed near its territory and now it needs you to pay.* Max didn't know where that thought came from, but he knew he was right. The body hadn't moved until he hit

(*disturbed*)

it, so he must have woken it up and caused it to attack. After it finished climbing in, the body of what once had been a jogger stood up, Max grabbed his oar, without thinking, and smacked its dead face.

Max's age didn't help him swing hard enough, but the jogger's neck snapped back with a wet cracking sound. The corpse turned back around and hissed, the white, dead eyes looking at him. It reached out with its odd, broken arms, and grabbed Max's throat, while he screamed. Its hands felt frigidly cold, as if it had crawled out of a freezer instead of a lake. With one final push of adrenaline, Max slammed into it, its grip loosened, and it fell back into the water.

It floated once more, in the position where he had found it. Max stayed standing and tense, expecting it to turn around and start climbing aboard again. He must've watched it for a full minute without looking away, until a bubble popped on the surface from where its mouth was facing the water. Its arms moved in its strange, broken fashion, and Max prepared to fight it off again. Only this time, it didn't grab on the boat, its arms flailed a bit, and it started to swim down towards the bottom of the lake.

The lake isn't glowing anymore. Max realized, before he came back to his senses. He grabbed both oars in his hands, and started to paddle away from the lake, back towards his home
(*I'll call the police they won't believe me but that's fine they'll search the lake and find the body, and it won't hurt anyone else*)
where he could rest and feel safe while the authorities dealt with whatever was going on.

Max's thoughts were interrupted when he realized his arms had frozen. No that's not it. The oars weren't moving, despite using all his strength to push them. Preparing what was left of his sanity, he looked over the side of the boat, and saw three pairs of white hands holding the oar to his right. What the hell? Max thought, as he quickly looked to the left oar, and saw two pairs of black hands holding the oar.
(*wait wait there's more there's fucking more*)

Another set of hands had held the oar in place, but these hands were different from the rest. These were a greenish color, and looked as though something had been nibbling at them. This body had obviously been there longer than the others had, the others still had a normal skin color, and no sense of decay had started in them.

Fear taking over, Max realized he may not be the first person exposed to this. He released the oars from his grip and started fondling the bottom of the boat for his filet knife
(*any weapon is better than nothing*)
as the bodies around his boat started to board.

There was a skinny white man, who looked a little deader than the others. A larger black woman and a smaller black man, who both looked preserved, but still as though the fish had nibbled a bit off. The rotten one came on board, he looked like an older man, and bits of skin on his face had fallen off to reveal the skull underneath. Finally, the jogger with the green shirt and iPod shoulder brace climbed up, letting out a hiss as its dead white eyes locked on to Max. The jogger's eyes were different this time, they were still pure white, but Max thought he saw something hateful in them this time. He quickly looked at the other creatures
(*bodies*)
on his boat and noticed the same glare in all of the white eyes.

They grabbed him, their ice cold hands gripping his body, and Max waited to be bitten or torn apart. He felt himself fall, and noticed his vision was blurry. He tried to breathe, and his nose filled with lake water.

(they pulled me under i can't break free, I can't breathe, what do I do oh my god what the fuck do I do)

The bodies dragged Max down, and the water beneath him felt colder with every foot they sank. He closed his eyes, he couldn't stand how bright the sun was at this moment, under all this water (*that's not the sun*) he realized for the second time that day.

He thought of how people see a bright light during near death experiences, and then he thought no more.

It looked like it was going to rain in an hour or two, but Sami decided she had time to canoe if she was quick. She grabbed her life jacket and her phone, promising herself she wouldn't drop it in the water, (a promise she wasn't sure she could keep, these days she had trouble remembering her lefts from her rights) and headed outside to the water.

Nobody else was on the lake, which was new. The lakes had been packed by tourists, but they had left a few days ago. *Some people still have to work*, she thought, laughing to herself. She sat in the canoe, and started to paddle.

Halfway across the lake, she heard something break above the surface of the water. She turned around and saw two men floating. The younger one had a neon green shirt, and the older one had a bright green vest on (*where did they come from I didn't see them before*).

She looked into her shirt pocket and pulled out her phone, but when she reached up to take a picture of the gruesome scene, the bodies had vanished.

What the hell? Am I losing it? Sami thought. *And why is the sun so bright today? It almost looks like I can see the bottom of the lake.*

Beneath the boat, far under the surface of the water, something began to stir.

Happiest Day

"What will the happiest day of my life be?" Little Lisa asked the old gypsy woman.

The woman smiled at the little girl, then gazed into her crystal ball. She looked mesmerized, and finally frowned. She looked back up at Lisa, who was beaming with anticipation.

"It'll be your wedding, little one." The gypsy said, with some reluctance.

Lisa lived anticipating that wonderful day. She fainted when her boyfriend proposed to her, as she knew that it meant her most perfect day was coming soon.

In the back of her mind, she had a little voice speak to her, telling her to get excited for her happiest day. It told her how to prepare, where the wedding should take place, what she could do to make it the best of all possible days.

It was everything she thought it would be. All her friends flew in to watch her get married. Her father managed to stagger out of his wheelchair to walk her down the aisle, while her mother had gotten out of bed after a long stint with a respiratory illness. Her dress was gorgeous, almost a bright shade of white, her husband looked more handsome than ever. She truly felt like the luckiest woman on the planet.

That's the thing about days, though. They only last 24 hours.

Lisa's mother died two years later, her lung collapsing. Her father lost his mind to Alzheimer's years after, alone in a nursing home she could hardly afford. Her friends had lost touch, as they each had spouses of their own, later their children dominated any free time they would have had to travel and visit Lisa. The voice in her head no longer told her things to look forward to, it just told her she had peaked. She had past her prime, and nobody needed her for their lives anymore.

Work was hard to come by since the pandemic hit. Schools were closed, so she could no longer teach the fourth grade. This hit her very hard, as even her fellow coworkers that had come to the wedding couldn't see her anymore. The voice told her they were relieved, that all their days would be brighter without her.

After months of listening to nothing but her inner voice, she stood at the edge of a, watching the wave below.

The voice told her to jump, and so she did.

The gypsy had been right, Lisa's wedding day would be the happiest day of her life.

But that left Lisa with a lifetime of nothing to look forward to, of days she'd always compare to her happiest one, never quite measuring up to that feeling of walking down the aisle, surrounded by loving friends and family.

If you ever get the chance to see your happiest day, pass it up.

Live your life as if you'll never know which day will be your best.

Because if you know, once it passes, what you're left with might not feel like enough.

The Family Dog

I have to get this story out there. I'm either losing my mind, or everything I write is actually happening, and I'm not sure which is more fucked up. I have to write all this down, because if I don't and something happens to me, nobody will know the truth, one way or another.

It started about a month ago, I lived with my parents and older brother. We were both in high school still, but our parents got high paying jobs, so we lived very comfortably at home. As much as I loved my parents and brother, I have to say our family dog was my best friend. Sometimes animals have a way of understanding us that other people never can come close to, and I'm not ashamed to admit that our golden retriever, Marley, got me through the tougher days of high school and teenage drama. Last month, that was all I had to worry about, now I'm not sure if I've gone insane.

It was one of those winter days where it gets dark as soon as you get home. My brother usually doesn't get home until after dinner, thanks to his leadership in our Robotics club, and my parents usually worked late, so I was the only one home. Marley came to enthusiastically greet me as I walked through the door, so I grabbed the box of Milk Bones from the kitchen to give him a treat. I asked him to do the usual tricks required for him to get his reward, and Marley obeyed quickly, excited at the prospect of what we called "cookies". I told him to sit, Marley sat. I told him to roll over, Marley rolled over. I told him to give me his paw, and screamed as Marley raised his paw, his human fingers wrapping around my own hand. I jumped back while Marley rushed forward to chomp on the treat, while looking up at me and wagging his tail. I leaned down, slowly, and looked at his front paws.

In place of little nails, my dog now had very hairy human fingers extending from his paws. I poked at them, and Marley recoiled, giving me the usual offended look he gives when I would try to grab his paws. He turned around and walked into the living room, his fingers making odd plopping sounds as they hit the hardwood floors in our kitchen. I followed him, and he curled up in the corner of the room, on his doggie bed we bought years ago, and watched me. Slowly I walked towards him, wanting another look at the fingers. They had to be a prank, my brother must've put them on him this morning or something. Laying down next to him, I grabbed his right paw to inspect it. The fingers didn't appear to be slipped on, they looked like they grew right out of his leg. The fingers curled up around my hand again, and I jerked my hand back as I heard a snarl. I got up quickly and looked down at my dog, Marley was baring his fangs at me, something I had never seen him do. He let out a low growl, and I backed off into my bedroom, locking the door, determined not to open it until my parents or brother came home.

My bedroom door opened almost as soon as I heard Mom's van door close. Marley started racing towards the door to greet her, although now his footsteps didn't sound familiar. I tried showing Marley's new development to her, but he would snap at me anything I got close to his fingers. Mom not only couldn't see his fingers, but took the dogs side for snapping at me, telling me not to touch his paws. I insisted and showed the fingers to her, and she gave me an odd look, before asking me if I was on drugs. After a heated argument, I had to agree to take a piss test, since I wouldn't back down on Marley's fingers. Angrily, I walked back to my room, but turned around when I heard Marley bark. He was staring at me, and I swear it was like he was smiling at me from down the hall. I slammed my door and tried to bury myself in homework. I ate dinner in my room, so I don't know what Mom told the rest of my family about the incident.

The next day I didn't see Marley when I woke up, although I spent my whole day at school dreading coming home alone for those few hours with just the dog. After convincing my friends, we went out for some after school custard, just so I could stay out of the house. I delayed them with stories and jokes as long as I could, but eventually we went our separate ways. I parked outside my house, and slowly walked inside, relieved that I only had to wait another ten minutes for Mom to get home.

Marley didn't come greet me, although I heard him get up and walk toward the kitchen. There was no enthusiasm, no tail wagging, nothing that dogs normally do when their owners come home. I saw the fingers first, and the rest of my dog followed them. I looked at

Marley, and noticed more changes, his face had sunken in, making his snout appear smaller, and his mouth was twisted in an odd, almost evil grin. I backed away, terrified, and Marley walked closer to me, which let me notice his fur was patchy in spots, letting his light pink skin show. He let out a few small growls, sounding almost like he was laughing at me. I won't lie, I turned and ran to my room, as Marley followed his fingers clipping on the floor behind me. I slammed the door just as he ran into it, and he began frantically scratching at the door. I yelled and yelled, and finally, he backed off. I heard him walk away, but stayed in my room again, afraid to go back out to those grinning teeth. Mom must've been running late, but when she came home, I was yelled at for tearing at my bedroom door. I explained that Marley had done that, but she didn't believe me, saying that he had never scratched anything in our house up before, and that he wasn't tall enough to scratch all of the door. Turning to look, I noticed that my bedroom door had long scrape marks going from the top to bottom, far too tall for Marley to have done, even if he had stood on his hind legs. After another argument, this time featuring my brother and dad, Mom decided to get me tested now, and after peeing in a cup, I had to wait a few days for results that I knew would come back clean. I stared at the ceiling that night, wondering if they would believe me once they knew I wasn't smoking pot.

The next few days passed normally, with one big exception. Marley never came to greet me when I came home. This was a relief, but it was short lived, as soon as I noticed his staring at me through the window, and watching me down the hall whenever I moved around. At times he would be grinning, his snout looking more and more flat, his teeth looking less and less pointed each day. His eyes were piercing, at night they looked like two small lights, following me in the darkness. Beyond watching me constantly, Marley behaved like a normal dog.

One night, I woke up from a bad dream. I grabbed the bottle of water next to my bed and took a big drink, before I noticed two glowing eyes watching me from the side of the room. I started screaming, waking my whole family up. Even though the drug test came back negative, they were still on edge with me, and were naturally upset at being woken up at two in the morning because the dog was in my room. I close my door every night, and my family knows this, so despite being angry at me so early in the morning, they did acknowledge it was weird that the dog got in my room. They figured I must've left it open, but I think I know the truth.

I think my dog used his fingers to open and shut my door so he could watch me sleep.

The next night I closed and locked my door. I didn't have school the next day so I stayed up late with my phone, hoping to catch Marley in the act and get a picture of him. Even though they couldn't notice his differences, a picture could show them Marley doing something impossible, and they would have to believe something was strange then. I heard footsteps down the hall, and my doorknob started to wiggle. I thought it was my brother, so I started to tell him to go away. As soon as I spoke, the wiggling stopped. I asked if my brother was there, but the only response was scratching. I sat in the corner of my bed, terrified. Finally, I saw a bloody finger burst through the door, followed by four more. The fingers gripped the hole in my door, and I quickly raised my phone and took a picture. I heard a deep snarl, and looked through the hole, seeing two furry, but very human eyes staring at me. Marley had scratched through my door just so he could watch me sleep. I took pictures, and although they weren't the best quality, they showed our dog had fingers, and was staring at me through the door. Sleeping would be impossible, so I spent the rest of the night staring back at what was once our dog, as he watched me with those hate filled eyes.

I must've drifted off at some point, because I woke up later to my parents yelling at Marley for scratching a hole in the door. They believed me now that I had not clawed at my own door days ago, but had no explanation for how Marley had. At my insistence, we went out to buy a new door for my room. After installing it, I noticed that it had no lock. Despite my begging, Dad would not go out and buy a new door after just attaching one, and my brother just told me to tie a sock to the door if I was going to "play with myself". I shot him my middle finger when my parents weren't looking, and we both laughed.

It was the last good moment I would feel, when I came home from school later that week, I waited in my car until Mom came home from work. I no longer felt safe in my own house, although I felt a slight comfort when the rest of my family was there with me. My nights were spent half awake, a kitchen knife tucked in under my pillow, ready to kill my own dog as if he tried to come into my room. The night before was no exception, and I was exhausted. Marley's human eyes were watching me from the living room window, his fingers pacing on the glass. As soon as Mom's car pulled around the corner, I started to get out. I made her walk in the house first, and from then on, the evening was normal. Later that night, I crawled into bed, feeling around for the knife.

"Looking for this?"

I turned around, and held back a scream. Marley was standing on almost human legs, still covered with tufts of fur. He was almost my height, and his face looked very much like an adult mans. The worst part was seeing my knife in my hands, his fingers wrapped around it. He sank back down and crossed his legs, still glaring at me with hatred. "Why?" It was all I could think to ask.

"You started to notice things," he said, his voice deep and disapproving, like a disappointed parent. "Nobody is supposed to notice what we are, and once they do they need to learn to keep their mouths shut."

I tried not to cry, I admit it. I couldn't scream, and I didn't know what to say, so all of my energy went to not bursting into fearful tears at the sight of my dog speaking to me.

He stood up again, and I flinched. He laughed. "You will leave me be, you will not try to explain to your family what I am, and you slowly you will forget, and return to your boring life." He stepped over to me, and I noticed he had feet on the bottom of his legs, not paws. "If you do not, I will tear you apart. I will rip your heart out and eat it. You'll die screaming, and when you do," he paused, "I will go to your mother, and I will kill her next, slower"

I didn't know what to do. Would anyone know what to do? This was fucking insane, I was speaking to my dog, Marley, who we had raised from a puppy. He had human limbs, and looked half human, but his eyes told me this wasn't just a human or a dog. This creature, this *thing*, our pet, was something else entirely. At that moment I knew this thing would kill me if I didn't agree. I nodded, and Marley began to laugh. He got back on all fours, and walked out of my room, his hands and feet smacking the floors on his way out.

I slammed the door, and grabbed a chair to hold it shut. I started writing this about a half hour ago, but Marley must have seen my light on. He has been clawing at my door for a few minutes, and I know he will eventually figure out there is no lock, I'm actually surprised it took him this long. I needed to write this down, because I lied. I can't live like this, I can't forget, and I think Marley knew that, and was going to attack me anyway. I thought about yelling to my family for help, but I didn't want them to get hurt too. Please, anyone reading this, just know I wasn't crazy in the end, you need to get rid of that dog, if he's still in the house.

I hear him, clawing, scratching, and even punching. My family must be sleeping through it, and I must admit it's funny that they failed to notice even this. I hope they'll be okay once I'm gone, I can see his fingers tearing through the wooden door, so I know I don't have much time. If my family finds this, get out and run. If anyone else finds this, get my family the fuck out of there. The doors broken down now I see it's staring at me his eyes are piercing why is he smiling ohmygo-

---

She didn't know what to do when she found her son's body besides cry. Someone had broken into their home, and attacked her son, whoever did it didn't even steal anything. Her husband and oldest son were a great comfort, although they, too, were destroyed by the sight. Her younger son's body parts were found all around the room, dark splotches of blood covered the carpet. The coroner said he must have died in agony, being torn apart by what must have been a large intruder. No normal person would have the strength to tear someone to shreds with their hands, like this intruder did. This bit of knowledge caused her to faint, and she woke up at home, resting on the couch. There was a note on the counter that her husband and son went out to speak to the police about anyone they could think of that would do this, and they would be back soon. She read the note, and wept. As if sensing her sadness, Marley came into the room, jumped on the couch, and rested his head on her lap. She smiled and pet him, wondering why her son was so afraid of him for the last month. He was a good dog, the kind that was always a comfort, always seeming to understand her in a way other people just couldn't.

She loved Marley, but didn't like the look in his eyes. His tail kept wagging, and he was relaxed, but his eyes looked unusual that day, as if she were looking at another person

Four Horsemen

Ironic that the beginning of the end would start quietly.

FAMINE came and went. Millions cried out, malnourished, while the others gorged themselves in their homes, thankful they were born lucky and privileged. So many that could have lived to change the world slowly starved instead. Their cries largely went ignored, as people assumed someone with authority could make the changes the poor needed.

PESTILENCE arrived second, in the form of a pandemic. The initial death toll was low, so not everyone took it seriously. Had they bothered to learn about the long term effects, things could have been different? Millions perished years after the outbreak, their lungs collapsing into soup. The bodies had to be burned to ensure the virus couldn't spread to a healthy host.

WAR was much louder than the others. With the total population on a decline, manufacturing became difficult, so resources became scarce. There were multiple conflicts for multiple resources, first a war for oil, then a war for food and water, most tragically was a war for freedom, as some of the poor had become slaves towards the end.

DEATH was final, by far the loudest, but the slowest of the four. The nukes took billions of lives when they coated the planet, but the fallout and radiation took so many more, over such a long time. For all its flaws, our once beautiful world was no longer hospitable, though people still tried to survive. Those unfortunate enough to survive this far had sickness and pain to look forward to. Many took their own lives when they had the opportunity, others survival instincts wouldn't let them, and they suffered on until their bodies couldn't any longer. The last human to die was a little boy, frightened and in great pain, wondering if he would see his mommy again.

It's easy to try to blame all this on divine intervention, a cosmic apocalypse, or even four mythical beings bringing destruction where they ride.

But the truth, the awful God damned truth of it all was much simpler.

There were no horsemen, there was no religious war, there was no higher power controlling our destiny.

There was only ever the kingdom of Man, and the choices that they made.

Stay with Me

"Isn't it breathtaking?"

"John, is that a pun?" He groaned, wrapping his arm around me. "But yeah, this is the most perfect view I've ever had."

We stared at the Earth. My husband and I were stationed on the moon, to collect samples and investigate some odd frequencies coming from the surface. It took a lot of convincing, but control let Brad and me team up for the mission. We were excited, we had met while training as astronauts, and despite the southern attitude surrounding us, we were an accepted, equal couple among our colleges.

"Down there, it matters to some people that we're together." Brad mused.

He was right. Up here on the moon it was silent. We were the only two living things, there was no judgement, no stress, and no fear. Our only concern was the mission.

Brad had me a little worried lately. He hardly slept and seemed more stressed than usual. I was trying to catch a nap while he tuned into the frequency. I heard him mumble for me a few times, but pretended to be asleep. Despite the fun of the mission, I was exhausted.

A few hours later, we were back outside, collecting more samples of moon rocks. I don't see what makes them so fascinating, they're just regolith after all, but the lab loves analyzing them.

"What?" I asked Brad for the third time. He kept whispering under his breath, and it was starting to get to me.

"Not talking to you." Brad said, looking worried.

I tried to shrug it off; mission first, relationship second, which had been the deal. But I kept hearing him talk through the radio, and finally I snapped.

"Dude what are you saying? Just talk to me instead of mumbling!" I yelled, harsher than I meant to.

Brad turned to me, I saw him grinning through his helmet. "She was telling me how to stay here with you for the rest of our lives."

"Hang on; she?" I asked, starting to get concerned.

Brad put his hand on the lunar surface, rubbing it like an animal. "The girl we came to investigate. I had to translate the signal, but when I did, she made it all clear. We can stay here, forever, away from judgmental pricks, weird glares at dinner, the stress of life on Earth."

Full panic. "Brad, there's no girl. Let's get you back to the ship, you need to sleep." I hoped that would be enough to settle him, or it'd be a long trip home.

He gave me a scared look. "No, don't get on the ship."

"What do you mean? We have t-"

Electricity burst from the ship. Pieces of it scattered, floating across the surface. Brad held up wires from the engine.

"I asked her, and she told me if the ship was gone, you and I could stay here with her. Forever."

Brad began to laugh hysterically as I watched our only ride home scatter across the surface. I sank to my knees, knowing any hope of rescue from control was floating away in our broken communication system.

Cult of the Great Iris

They called themselves the Cult of the Great Iris, and nobody took them seriously.

Cults have a negative connotation, but the Cult of the Iris seemed harmless, and was protected under religious law. Its members joined voluntarily, and were free to leave at any time, although very few did. Those that left often did so because they had children, and wanted to raise them outside of the cult. True to their word, these people were let free, with no repercussions. Some even came back after their children had grown up.

That should have been the first clue.

A large number of child kidnappings were eventually connected to the group. One member had gotten sloppy, and was caught in broad daylight trying to abduct a seven year old girl. The member himself didn't give up any information, other than they had been abducting one child every year for the past three centuries, far longer than official records indicated regarding the cult's existence.

Former members who had not returned were brought in for questioning, all but one woman withholding any more information. She only gave in because the officer threatened to- well, I'm not going to write that. It was a huge scandal, and I hate to say it, but the police got the information they needed, including the cult's real location.

Turns out, the cult believed that unless one child under the age of nine was skinned alive above a metal plate, a giant red eye would descend from the heavens, and obliterate the Earth. This story dominated the news, many parents of missing children connected to the case finally had closure, but at the cost of hope for their child's safe return, or at least a quick end.

Those that they arrested were put in padded cells, where they screamed and yelled that their Eye would be coming soon unless they could stop it.

A giant, red symbol appeared in the sky during the night. It looked like it was made out of flame, and, despite being positioned over Asia, it was visible across the whole planet. Nobody knew what it meant, so they interrogated a cult member.

The symbol was the same as the one over the metal grate, the member claiming it was Cuneiform for the number three. Why Cuneiform, and not a Native American script, was never understood, but the member claimed they had three days to skin their kid, or the Eye would come.

The next day, the symbol changed, becoming the Cuneiform number two.

Astronomers noticed another anomaly. Jupiter had decreased in size, and a giant storm of energy was rushing towards Earth.

Jupiter's red eye was gone, and was coming towards us.

I stand in the bunker, a knife in hand and a neighborhood girl tied to the rack.

The Cuneiform number for one was broadcast in the sky this morning.

I don't have enough time to weigh my odds. I close my eyes, and get ready to do what must be done.

The Ritual

I work for a psychological clinic in Northern Wisconsin, in the backwoods area where the closest city has a population of 3000 people.

Billy came to me after having a nightmare, about an old man named Rick who lived in an old cabin down the block. Billy says in the dream, neighbor Rick brought him into the cellar, where five weird creatures were sitting, chanting.

He described them as human shaped, but with deer skulls for heads. Their eye sockets were empty, but Billy could feel them hate him when they turned to look at him.

I asked him what happened next, he broke down crying. I told him it was okay if he needed a break, and we could pick up next week.

I got more nervous when my next client claimed to have a weird dream, involving a man named neighbor Rick.

She described the exact same dream as Billy, Rick taking her to the cellar, deer skull creatures in a circle. This time I asked her what they were circling, but she just mumbled "Rick" and broke down to tears just like Billy did.

I had four more clients that day, and three of them described the exact name nightmare, although none could tell me what the creatures were circling.

I knew which cabin they were talking about, they all described the abandoned pioneer cabin down by the outskirts of town. The sun was setting, so I drove there quickly, assuming some creep was squatting, and scaring curious children. I had never dealt with repressed memories before, and probably should've just called the cops, but I had to see for myself. Maybe they all watched the same scary movie or something.

The cabin reeked. It smelled the way people's garages do around hunting season, when they gut and hang their deer up. I got out my flashlight, gasping as it illuminated bloody symbols on the wall.

Rushing back to my truck, I got my hunting rifle out, slamming the clip inside. Confident I could shoot if I needed to, I went down into the cellar.

There knelt five man sized things, the deer skulls dragging on the ground as they bowed to a bloody figure. Slowly, the figure turned and sat up, and had the look of a grizzled, middle aged man.

"They cursed me…." He mumbled, the creatures standing up. "Left me... without a body… but I got their ancestors to... see the truth….they brought me back."

I don't know what those kids saw, how any of this works, or what it means, but it brought an old, dead, apparently evil pioneer back from the grave. I escaped, rushing out the door, and contacted the families, but they couldn't find their kids.

I called the police, who finished their investigation by the morning. No sign of a man named Rick, but they did find the five missing kids. Or rather, their bodies, all tied together. Attached to all five of their necks were old deer skulls.

Northwood's Retreat

Thank you for visiting our rental cabin in Rohr village! We hope you enjoy all that the Northwood's of Wisconsin has to offer. There are some rules you should follow during your stay, and for your convenience we have them listed right here.

1. When fishing in the lake, do not pull up anything that feels too heavy to be a fish. They are not a big catch, and they will drag you down with the rest of them.
2. If you see hunters with no face wearing blaze orange, shoot them on site. Do not let them get close enough to touch your face. If you accidentally shoot a normal hunter, we will compensate you for your stay.
3. The bodies in the cellar are not real, don't call the police. They won't be able to see them, and they're sick of "prank calls"
4. The boat can be used as much as you want, although blood stains cannot be removed. Avoid them as much as possible, as they are contaminated with lymes disease.
5. Cook what you catch/kill, and burn any remaining garbage. Any wasted food will attract the local bears. The bears are generally docile, but if you see any with human eyes, do not try to speak to them, no matter what they say.
6. If the power goes out, do not panic, but do not light any candles or use any flashlights. The wendigo that cut the power cannot see in the dark.

7. Bring a tent and supplies for an overnight trip if you hike near the property. If you wander off the trail, it'll be at LEAST one night before you find your way back.

8. The local cult is annoying, but generally harmless. They believe in some fish god that lives in the lake, which is also annoying but harmless. If they're grilling out, go ask to join them. The meat they make is fantastic.

9. There is no reception this far up north, any calls or texts that you get on your phone should be ignored.

Enjoy your stay at Rohr village! We hope you leave feeling refreshed and filled with the spirit of the woods!

Island Rules

Hello, I'm hoping nobody will ever have to read this, but I wanted to write it up while I still have enough sanity to do so. My name isn't important, and if you are opening this journal, who I am is the least of your concerns.

We were fighting those fucks from Japan, and we got shipwrecked on an unknown island. There were twelve of us when we first got here. Now I'm the only one left, and I don't know how much time I have. I wanted to write down the rules of this island, to give anyone who reads this a fighting chance. They are as follows

- The sun rises and sets at odd times, we tried and failed to find any pattern, sometimes it's up for days, and night time can last weeks.
- If you are with anyone that dies, DO NOT bury them. They crawl out of the ground and try to talk to us at night. Burn the bodies instead.
- The pale naked woman that wanders around spends most of her time crying. She will leave you alone if you leave her alone, but **do not** try to comfort or communicate with her in any way.
- I could not read the words engraved on the trees, but one of my fellow soldiers was able to. He chewed through his wrists and bleed out moments after telling us he understood them. None of us have any desire to try to translate it, and I would advise anyone reading this should avoid them, just to be safe.

- The fruit that drops from the trees is safe to eat, although it does give you a "high" feeling, as if you know everything about the world and are at peace with it. A side effect is that the feeling becomes somewhat addictive. One of my friends here ate too much too quickly, and has been staring at the ocean for the past 5 days without moving. Try to find other food if possible, as of now I have not found anything else, and have been eating my fellow soldier's bodies to avoid the temptation of the fruit.

- If you recognize someone on this island that you did not arrive here with, absolutely do not attempt to contact them in any way. If they approach you, do your best to ignore them, no matter how angry they get. They are not the person you think they are, and from what we can of the bodies they leave behind, they kill you slowly if you acknowledge them.

- Some nights you will wake up in a cabin away from the shoreline. When this happens, stay awake all night, do not open the doors for any of the people that will knock, and do not leave the cabin until the sun is out. When you leave the cabin, you will not be able to find it again. Nobody from our group has woken up there twice, so stay calm and collected and you should be okay.

- Do not sing, or even hum, once the sun is down. If you hear singing anywhere on the island, drop what you are doing and walk the other way until you cannot hear it anymore.

- The birds are not safe to eat. If you eat one, the rest will follow you. Do not let them catch you.

- The smaller man that appears sometimes calls himself Isaac, and is friendly. He will be kind and help you survive, but will become agitated if you ask him about the island, the metal that's warped on his skin, or the words engraved on his head. Do not let him near your food, as it decays when he touches it.

Addiction

The brain adapts to constant use of a substance, adjusting neurotransmitters as the addiction goes on. When a person stops using a substance, their brain is left with too much and too little amounts of neurotransmitters, making them crave the substance to feel level. This is commonly referred to as "withdrawal".

One dose of heroin and I was hooked. I wasted so many years of my life alone and in pain, just waiting for the next hit, knowing eventually that high would fizzle away and I'd be left shivering and waiting again.

I was homeless.

I've been robbed more times than I can count.

I've lost fingers to frostbite.

Muscle atrophied as I stopped caring about exercise.

I was arrested twice, spent time in a jail going through withdrawal while being mocked by the officers.

My rock bottom was robbing a convenience store. I only had a pocket knife, waving it frantically and charging through the doors at 3 in the morning.

I never wanted to hurt the kid, but I knew I'd saw him in half if it meant I could have another fix.

He panicked, and tried to run. His panic brushed off on me, and I slashed forward, opening his throat.

I grabbed the whole register and bolted, hearing pained gurgling behind me.

The next day I checked into rehab.

I found a purpose again, I helped other addicts figure out the root problems they had, and how they could overcome their addiction. I liked to think the good I accomplished outweighed the bad, but morality isn't a measurable quality.

Reconnecting with my family and friends was horrifying, but I persevered. Without their love and support, I wouldn't have been able to power through my own recovery.

Because of them, I got my life back.

The one thing I never did was talk about the convenience store. I know I should have, it would have felt good to get it out of me, but I didn't have it in me to look anyone in the eye and try to excuse what I did.

I wish I was sorry for not being stronger. Maybe things would have turned out different.

I woke up in a cell, with a wicked hangover. Adrenaline flooded my veins; did I relapse last night? I noticed a note next to the bed, and began to cry after reading it.

That kid's father had owned the store. He kept the tapes, never reporting me, keeping tabs on me for years, watching me recover. He spent savings on supplies; bunker, needles, water bottles and snacks, and finally, heroin.

I've been staring at the crate for days. I know he's watching, he won't let me out until I use again, and then I'll be hooked again.

I finally got my life back under my control.

But it's only a matter of time before the urge takes control again.

I don't want to go back to that life.

Please God, don't make me go back.

Would You Die For Me?

I repeated the question to Kevin when his answer was stunned silence. It was just him and I, our usually Friday date night had been soured with the news that my cancer had spread. I had weeks of chemotherapy and radiation treatment to look forward to.

Kevin was, well, hot. He had short hair, a thick beard, a little beer belly on an otherwise physically fit body. It was unfair for me to feel bad, he told me himself, but there was still so much regret at the idea that I couldn't be beautiful for him. My hair would fall out, I'd be throwing up, dark circles would overtake my eyes, and I'd lose too much weight.

Part of me whispered he would leave when it got to that point, so I asked him the question. He wrapped his arm around me, my face flushed as I felt him squeeze me tighter than ever before. "Of course, Sophie." He answered, looking me right in the eyes.

I felt at peace. "I love you." I reminded him, leaning into his soft but muscular chest. "Are you sure, though? You'd really die if it meant I could live?"

He stared at me again, his guard down and love flowing from his eyes. "If I could take your cancer out of you and put it inside me, I would."

I sighed, a little disappointed. "I looked into alternative medicine, the woman gave me one treatment plan, but I needed your permission first."

"What kind of permissio-" Kevin stops as I quickly slash his throat. He grasps his neck, putting pressure on the wound, but it won't help him. I got the carotid artery and his trachea, either he would bleed to death or suffocate.

He lay on the carpet, groaning as I held him down and tore his chest open. His eyes are filled with betrayal, and for a moment I feel guilty. It had to be by surprise, Kevin wrestled in college, and I only weighed 120 pounds soaking wet, I wouldn't have been able to subdue him any other way.

I reached into his chest, ripping out his heart from the attached arteries and connective tissue. The witch had said I had to take a bite while it was still beating, so I quickly jammed it into my mouth while Kevin let out his death rattles, giving me a confused, sorrowful glance.

I try not to feel too bad about it. She was right, the display of betraying someone completely loyal to me was enough, the cancer faded away within a week. Doctors were baffled, I claimed it must have just been a miracle. I told the police I didn't know what happened to Kevin, I cried at his funeral, playing the part of the victim very well.

I should feel bad, but I don't.

After all, he did tell me he'd die for me, right?

The Big Freeze

You think absolute zero is a theoretical concept?

Guess again, idiot.

Absolute zero is the temperature when, measured in Kelvin, matter produces no vibrational motion, and atoms stand completely still. I don't have time to simplify it more than that, you probably wouldn't understand even if I did.

For years, researchers like myself have been trying to understand how quantum mechanics can handle a zero energy state. We've gotten close a few times, trying to get the temperature of various metals as low as possible.

My team achieved this on February 10th, 2021.

The first intern we lost was the closest to the room. He was following the group outside to get a celebratory drink when he suddenly stopped moving. My friend grabbed his shoulder, and also stopped moving. We quarantined the site, but by now I think you're smart enough to see where this goes.

You may have noticed some big cold fronts coming in lately. Hell, here in [REDACTED] it's been hovering at -20°F all day, getting colder by an average of 1.2°F each day. (I know you Americans like to fetishize Fahrenheit, I figured I'd save you the time of googling a conversation factor.)

We caused that. The substance we got down to absolute zero worked, but caused a previously unseen quantum phenomena. Turns out, quarks are like people, in a way. They act independent when it suits them, but in reality they need stimuli from each other. Temperature, pressure, velocity changes are all measured on an individual level, but influenced by the surrounding quarks.

For those of you who failed chemistry and physics in college, this matters because if quarks received zero energy from their surroundings, they also might switch to that low energy state. I really can't dumb it down more than that, not in 500 words, which is all this terminal will allow in one document. The point is, we created an infection of absolute zero, and it's slowly spreading across individual quarks.

Yes, the world really is getting colder. Soon, it'll be frozen. Not just frozen in ice, but completely frozen; a world where mass has no meaning, light cannot travel, consciousness is frozen in one spot, with one thought, for all eternity.

Once my theory was confirmed on the news, I poisoned my family. I didn't want them to think "Daddy, I'm cold" forever.

It's been suppressed by now, stupid governments decided people don't need to know their upcoming, inescapable fate, while they raced to build heat bunkers to attempt survival.

Rich morons, all of them. Absolute zero can't be stopped by walls, no matter what they're composed of.

They can't suppress the cold front, though, and I'm sure by now most of you are smart enough to notice it's a preternatural cold. For what it's worth, I'm sorry. I never thought science could go far enough, and now we caused the heat death of the universe.

Eventually, all existing matter will sit absolutely still. Starting with us.

Stay warm.

 Alone

The biggest problem I had with society is that other people lived in it.

I'm not a big fan of other people, you see. I liked to keep to myself, sleep alone in a big bed, come home after work and just decompress in the silence. But other people always had to try to worm their way into my life, thinking they could break down my walls or get to know me better.

There's not much to know, and that was never their fault. I simply preferred to be left alone.

I moved into a recluse cabin years ago. Technically, it wasn't even on a map. Perfect for a guy like me. I could sit on my porch and drink coffee, go for a long walk in the forest, just enjoy the silence and solitude. Alone at last

I watched the news sometimes, however. I didn't want to be completely gone from the real world, just a little….detached from it, let's say. I realized I didn't hate other people, I just preferred if they would leave me alone.

They came quickly and without warning, giant balls of light and eyes sank down from the skies above. The words BE NOT AFRAID were pressed into everyone's heads, and about a fourth of the population flew upwards with the things.

They never came back down.

I sat in my cabin, worried about what this all meant. Nobody could understand what had happened, although the main theory was that the rapture had begun. Alone in my isolated cabin, I wasn't impacted by the looting or rioting that followed, although I was still impacted by the fear of this unknown.

The other side came a few days later. They crawled up from the ground, large black horned creatures with fire in their eyes. News footage showed people running away, before being dragged screaming into the ground by the creatures.

It didn't take long after that for the news to cut out, and soon after that the power cut out altogether.

Whatever happened to everyone, it didn't happen to me. I don't know how, or why, but both sides seemed to ignore me, if the rapture theory was to be believed. If it was truly Heaven and Hell coming to claim humanity, they left me behind, neither side claiming me.

I walked outside my cabin, a warm cup of coffee in my hands. Conflicting emotions got the best of me, and as I breathed a sigh of relief, hot mournful tears began to flood through my eyes.

Alone at last.

Answers

My friend had a gift. Anytime someone asked him a question, he immediately knew the answer, no matter what it was.

He confided this ability to me after college, explaining his phenomenal grades that appeared in sharp contrast to his lack of effort, we decided to use the ability to-what else? Get rich.

I asked him to solve complicated mathematical equations that were thought to be impossible, and he wrote them out in a notebook in a trance. I asked what the lottery numbers for next week would be, and he told me while we drove to the gas station near our apartment.

When I asked him how to cure cancer, he got a nose bleed. Apparently, he now had chemical and radiological solutions to cure any type of cancer, but the range of answers appearing in his mind caused him great strain. Apparently this ability had a weakness, or at least some limitations, and we decided to be more careful with the phrasing of questions.

Years later, we were both rich, living in our own mansions. He needed me to ask him questions, the ability didn't work without it, and so we agreed to split the difference evenly. Also, why not? We could hypothetically do whatever we wanted, so if either of us ran low on cash, we'd just figure out how to solve a world problem in the simplest way, and get rich off it.

Poverty, infection, and hunger rates worldwide were at an all-time low. The world was a much better place, because of us. Well, mostly my friend, but you get the gist.

We went out to celebrate the breakthrough in interstellar travel, something that took years of nosebleeds, headaches, and carefully curated questions to answer. We picked a college bar from our old school, wanting to live up to the old times.

Unfortunately, we were a lot more stupid back then, and being back in our old stomping grounds brought back that familiar air of carefree actions.

The lack of inhibition, both from alcohol and other drug consumption, caused me to forget our rule of careful questions, and led me to drunkenly ask my friend what happens after we die.

Almost immediately he began screaming, his nose spurting blood like a firehouse over the bar floor. He slammed his head on the bar over and over again, until his face was bloody and broken. He ran behind the bar, knocking the barkeep over and grabbing an empty bottle, before smashing it against the wall. We made eye contact for a brief moment, where I saw the view of a man weathered and aged by centuries of pain.

He slashed the bottle across his throat. His screaming stopped while the other patrons began to panic and scream for themselves.

Standing among the pandemonium in the bar, for the first time in years, I had nobody to ask what would happen next.

Secrets

In order to convey a thought to another, a person must first conceive a speech, produce sound waves from their throat, and expel those waves out of their mouth. A second person must have these waves hit their ear, becoming chemical signals in response to stimuli, and then translate these effects into the original thought.

This is obviously a quick version of the physics of communication. Imagine this is the barrier that allows human beings to maintain our own thoughts, consciousness, ideas, and secrets. Without this, humans would not be individuals, they would be books, waiting to be read by anyone who can translate them.

Gustavus, Alaska is a town of 442 people, according to the 2010 census. Now, in 2021, that number is closer to 50 or 60.

The barrier allowing for individual thought thinned one day. Townsfolk no longer had to speak to communicate, they could convey ideas to others just by thinking about. Spontaneously, telepathy had become reality, but only inside the border of this small town.

Teachers taught their small classes simply by thinking of the processes they would otherwise need to explain. Toddlers could think about symptoms, removing the guesswork from a difficult diagnosis.

Sometimes the people we feel closest to are the ones that are the hardest to talk to, but people were finally able to admit the things they never knew how to put to words.

The barrier kept thinning, more and more. People assumed they were improving on their telepathic communication, until they began accidently communicating things they swore never to speak of. Nobody knew how to turn it off, how to hide their own thoughts, or how to stop reading others thoughts. Groups became isolated from each other to avoid "overhearing", but over time, the whole town became a humming chorus of dark secrets.

"john you are timmy's real father i'm sorry i lied to you."

"cheating on caroline for three years now and i just can't stop."

"hit a little girl with my car a decade ago left her to die see her at night when i dream killed someone."

Scattered confessions hit every citizen, some were unable to handle what they heard.

Cuckolds were chasing their wives down the street, murder in their eyes.

Families were torn apart, some devolving into group suicide.

Local politicians were executed once corruption became public knowledge.

Within four months after the barrier fell, Gustavus had eaten itself, bodies buried in mass graves. Those that tried to leave found they spread the condition with them, so the remaining citizens agreed to quarantine in Gustavus, to let everyone else keep their secrets; after all, they had seen what happens when they get out.

John, a former drug addict, wrapped himself in his coat, shivering from the cold. Sally, who had beaten her son to death while he cried, walked the dog. They waved at each other, both convincing themselves they were happy, content with where they are.

To keep any peace, they have to be.

What Happens After

The first time I died I was in college. I crossed the road without looking at a drunken stupor and got railed by a pickup truck. Totally my fault; that time hurt quite a lot. I felt bones shatter, ribs punctured lungs, and finally a dark wave of nothing washed over me.

Then I woke up to a horn blaring, and the truck swerving out of the way.

It took me some time to figure it out. So there's this multiverse theory, right? An infinite number of universes, all next to each other, only slightly different than the last. Always some constants, but different variables in each one; the year your home country became independent, how long it took people to reach the moon, if they did at all, different civilizations collapsing a lot sooner or later.

How long someone will live.

I've deduced that every time someone dies, their consciousness slips into a different one of these infinite universes, where they survive their death. They just don't remember it, they just live on, and the only variable in the new universe is that their life goes on as normal.

But for some reason, I can remember dying, and I know that I'd just move to an identical universe and live on. Effectively, we were all immortal, but I seemed to be the only one who knew it.

I had to experiment with this a few times. (Wouldn't you?) Each time after I died, I would wake up moments later, with no physical damage done to my body, life went on. Sometimes it hurts during, but it's a small price to pay to live free.

I lived my life without fear from that point on. I went skydiving, rock climbing, scuba diving, any extreme sport that could result in my death.

Bad things happened all the time, my parachute wouldn't deploy, I'd miss a ledge and plummet, my oxygen tank would burst and I'd drown.

But every time I'd wake up and everything would be fine.

The most recent time didn't feel any different. I actually wasn't doing anything exciting, just flying on a plane to visit my parents for the holidays. I have no idea why, but the plane went down, taking all the passengers with it.

I woke up again, confused by why it was so dark. There was no light around me at all. I thought maybe I had covered my face on the flight, but there was nothing to pull off.

I've been waiting for decades now. Time feels slower, in the time it took you to read this, it's felt like three months for me. It takes too long to form coherent thoughts, like I'm constantly intoxicated. No matter how long I wait, I don't seem to wake back up on the plane. This isn't death, I can still form thoughts, just scattered and slow.

Every time someone dies, their spirit travels to a parallel universe where they live.

But I think I missed it this time.

Blood type:

Inconclusive

I stared at the patient's chart. He had been an organ donor, and we needed to know his blood type, in addition to other details, to avoid rejection by a healthy host.

I don't let sleeping dogs lie, I needed to know the type.

To summarize, some blood types have different antibodies and antigens, which means if you give someone the wrong type, the immune system will attack itself. Which is, generally, a bad thing.

This guy's blood though, it...kept changing its expressed antibodies and antigens. I mixed it with other samples we had in the lab, but whether the blood was A, B, or O, no immune response was produced.

This man had a blood type that adapted to the blood around it.

I had a great track record in blood bank from then on as a med tech. Anytime we had a trauma, I always had the correct type of blood ready to go. Nobody used the bottom draw in the cooler, so I kept a small supply of the blood, which I called "Type C", down there.

Sometimes I'd dilute it with extra blood, or even expired blood, but it always retained its same immune properties, no matter how diluted the original sample got.

Every patient we had recovered with no complications, even faster than an ordinary person would. I was a hero, and I didn't have to prove why.

Of course, good things don't last forever, and in the end, we all get caught.

There was a series of gruesome murders, mostly in the cities around our hospital. Victims were found with slashed throats and wrists, with bite marks around the cuts. Not completely drained of blood, but the implication was that the killer had drunk from them.

The investigators learned that the killers, who all eventually got caught roaming the streets, had all had a trauma recently, which led them to learn they all had a blood transfusion recently, which led them to our hospital, which led them to my name, which was listed in our blood bank for every single one of procedures.

I came clean almost immediately, and even though I was absolutely fired and in trouble with the law, they let me help investigate Type C.

Turns out, Type C blood can always adapt to a new host, as long as it has a different blood type to feed on and transform. The patients were fine, for a time, but after a while, Type C converted all of their blood, and needed new, fresh blood to corrupt. Hence the feeding.

The next problem was that all of the victims' bodies had vanished from the morgue, a decent amount of mortician bodies found dead in the same way.

The road to Hell is paved with good intentions, I suppose.

I accidentally started a vampire outbreak.

My bad, guys. :/

The Witch House

Deep in the forests of northern Wisconsin, there's an old, abandoned cabin, where a witch used to live.

If you travel over the river and through the woods (seriously? To grandmother's house we go?) You'll find it, and possibly be inclined to explore it.

Don't.

If you step inside, you'll never walk more than a mile away from the cabin again. No matter which direction you walk, you'll always end up back at that cabin.

The longer you spend there, the more you'll forget yourself. Your dreams, hobbies, emotions, memories, all become part of the cabin.

Each time this happens to a traveler, the cabin gets a little nicer, looking less abandoned and more neglected.

After a few days you'll start to see someone following you around. You'll think it's a hallucination, brought on by hunger or thirst, but you won't feel either of those things. At least, not to the level that you should.

If you get close enough to the figure, you'll notice it looks a little like yourself.

Small details are off, eye color, hair length, but after a few more days, the figure will correct itself, starting to look exactly like you.

If you look in a mirror, you'll notice you look like a dried out husk of what you used to be.

Or maybe that's just because you lost the memory of what you looked like by now. After all, you'd have been at the cabin for almost a week.

The doppelgangers used to be terrible. They wouldn't know how to act once they left the forest, and almost all of them would either end up killing themselves or become institutionalized, mumbling about how "She" wants them back.

The witch takes power from lonesome travelers, you see. That's why the cabin takes your memories, your essence, and finally, your form. She uses a little bit of this energy to copy you, and send that copy back into the real world, to avoid suspicion. She's getting better at it, through trial and error, to the point where if you live in Wisconsin, chances are you know at least one person who isn't what you think they are. She's gotten good at replicating people by now, and disposing of the remains of the original.

Despite being only alive as a spirit, she's not stupid.

At this point, the cabin looks livable. Only a few cracks on the windows, few holes in the walls, just a bit of a fixer upper, compared to the abandoned hut it used to be just years ago.

You wouldn't know there were hundreds of dried out bodies buried underneath it.

If you know someone who comes back from a trip up north, and they start acting a little off, do not follow them the next time they go for a hike. Do not ask them about the cabin, or about Her, maybe just cut them off completely.

Recently, the doppelgangers have started trying to bring people back to that place.

And they're getting a little more efficient every time.

Fake News

It's my body, my freedom, and my choice to have my family over for Christmas.

We've celebrated every holiday together this year, despite people complaining to us.

"You're gonna get people sick!" So what? I'm healthy and it's basically just the flu.

All this fake news makes my blood boil. Shutting down the country? Over a virus? What do scientists know anyway? They're still insisting on climate change, and it snowed just last night!

We did everything together, I drove into town to celebrate my mom's birthday; she just turned 58 a few months ago, but she doesn't feel "at risk" at all! We all gathered at my brothers for the 4th of July, sharing cigars and launching fireworks from our backyard.

Thanksgiving I got angry. I was so sick of these restrictions, people telling me what to do, how to wear my mask, where I can and cannot go.

People laughed at me when I told them my entire family was coming over for Thanksgiving, they called me stupid, uneducated, selfish; any of the buzzwords people use nowadays to make you stop thinking for yourself.

They were all wrong. In fact, they spent the night in my guest rooms, I hadn't slowed rent collection for my tenants in the building I owned, so I spared no expense upgrading to a nicer home this year, full of extra rooms and private bathrooms.

Christmas was easy to plan for, after all, my family was still over from Thanksgiving.

I set out plates for everyone gathered around the table. They were hard to lift, but I got everyone seated comfortably. I ask if anyone would like to say Grace, and they all just look at me blankly.

The ham I made was great, but nobody seemed into it. In fact, I'm wondering if I should turn the heat up, everybody feels so cold lately. They all got a little sick before, but once they stopped coughing I knew they had recovered just fine, as I predicted. This little virus wasn't that big of a deal, it just made everyone kind of quiet. Plus, they stopped cleaning up so well, they smell a little.

I picked everyone up and set them around the couch, giving Dad the big recliner he likes. My Mom was slouched over, but I think she just had a little too much wine with dinner. That might be my fault, I was practically pouring it onto her.

My brother and sister share the futon, each leaning on the other. They need to get outside more, they both look so pale. The news comes on, displaying that fake death toll they keep rattling about. I laugh with my family, knowing it was exaggerated.

After all, my family got sick for a little, but they all pulled through. It really wasn't that bad.

The media has a bias, they tend to exaggerate these things.

"Merry Christmas." I tell my family, and for a second I almost hear them whisper it back.

Ice Fishing

The underwater camera had great quality, Jake was glad he had treated himself to a more expensive version than his last one, despite losing his job a month ago.

He had three tip ups around him, and one pole in his hand. The bottom of the lake was displayed on screen against his cooler, showing fish swimming past his bait, sometimes leaning in for a quick smell, before slinking away into the darkness.

Dammit, Jake thought, seeing a small school ignore his hooks. Suddenly a small dark form emerged from the sand. Jake let himself get excited, the time had finally come for him to catch something today! He leaned in to observe the screen, before noticing the form was gripping at empty water with its fingers.

Fingers?

Jake leaned in closer. What he thought was a fish resembled a human hand, moving around in the murky bottom of the lake. Jake recoiled, but couldn't turn away from the screen, noticing that the remaining arm began to emerge from the muck as well.

The camera feed displayed a figure swimming upwards past it, and out of site. If the figure crawled out in front of the camera, that would place it...Jake darted away from the hole he had drilled, but the hand still reached out and gripped his ankle, attempting to pull him underwater. He thrashed and struggled, not unlike a fish out of water, before his leg was dragged into the hole, a loud crack echoing across the ice as his tibia snapped in half from the angle it was bent at.

Jake screamed, realizing the only thing keeping him above water was the ice. Using more force than he thought he had, he pulled himself and his damaged leg free from the things grip, dragging himself away from the hole with a loud shriek. The pain was awful, Jake reached for his phone but the screen stayed off. His phone was damaged from the water, and the pocketknife he brought must have sank.

Under the ice, a large dark figure was swimming around, circling the area Jake was hobbling over. The thing was larger than the camera had shown, and although he couldn't determine its exact shape, it looked like a large eel with human appendages.

Jake heard the creature below from under the ice, before crashing up. The ice around him began to splinter and crack, cold water rising up in the puddle around him. Jake slowly began to sink as the ice under him broke up, unable to hold his weight. He tried to crawl, but the pain in his leg stopped him. Whatever fight or flight instincts people talked about didn't appear to be kicking in for him.

The creature was looking at him, its mouth open wide with rows of jagged teeth. He noticed a human emotion in its slimy eel eyes.

Hatred.

Jake could only whimper as the cold water enveloped him,

sliding him into the creatures open maw.

Winter Camping

Greg thought he was prepared for a weekend of solo winter camping, and he would have been, if a sudden blizzard didn't roll in overnight.

He cursed the weather app on his phone, battery now dead from the cold, for telling me it would be light flurries at worst. His tent had caved under the snow, and it took him much longer than he wanted to pack up camp and turn around.

It didn't take him long at all to get lost. Everything around him was a blank, white sheet.

Greg swore again, out loud this time, and set up camp for another night, curling up in a ball and shivering.

He woke up to a figure standing outside his tent door. He sighed with relief on realizing it was just a snowman, but wondered who had set one up in the night? The blizzard had covered any tracks around the tent, so he couldn't even tell which direction they had gone.

After following his compass for another day, Greg was forced to set up camp for a third night, wondering how he would explain this to his boss.

This time there was more than one snowman, five, to be precise. The snow had lessened, but Greg could still not find any tracks around his tent, not even his own. He forced himself to remain calm, as nothing productive would come from panicking.

He let himself feel fear later that night when he had to set up camp again, this time keeping watch to see who was messing with him in the woods.

Greg didn't fall asleep, but when the sun rose, he noticed an uncountable number of figures sounding his tent. All were snowmen, no tracks around the tent, and they seemed to stretch for miles.

Panic took over. Greg kicked at one of the snowmen, screaming and swearing. The figures had frozen more overnight, so the snowmen did not budge. Angrily, Greg brought his axe out, and slashed off one of their heads.

He screamed again when blood splattered over the snow.

The snowmen around him screeched, and began to shuffle through the snow toward him. Greg shivered, and held his axe defensively, but stick like arms reached up from the headless snowman to hold him in place. The snowmen began to throw snow at Greg, some of them rushing forward and hitting him with it. He felt his body temperature decrease, unable to even scream for help and a snowman forced snow into his open mouth. He died with a feeling of warmth, despite his skin turning black from frostbite.

The authorities were baffled. They found the missing person deceased, but with no motive as to what killed him.

The man, Greg, had been dismembered, his arms sticking out of one giant snowball, legs jutting out from the lower one, resembling a grotesque snowman. His head, cheeks red and lips blue, sat atop the figure, a frozen scream stuck to his face.

Solo Camping

Being able to see what feels like EVERY star in the sky, a bottle of beer in one hand and a funky cigarette in the other, around a warm fire. You feel so small, but so focused. It helps wipe the sludge of everyday life away.

Being surrounded by people and having to act like the person they know you as is draining. I need to be able to completely remove the mask, with nobody around to see it. A huge weight is lifted, I don't have to be anyone, I'm not a lab tech, I'm not a white middle class man, I'm not anything other than a man visiting nature, and I love it.

The "incident" changed my feelings. There was rustling outside my tent, small little giggles. I slowly rolled over, grabbing both my flashlight and pistol, and charged out of the tent at whatever was harassing me, pointing my gun right at a dark shape scrambling around.

I always tell my friends where I'm camping. This time, however, they thought it'd be funny to come prank me at night. I got in a big shouting match with the three of them, upset both because they betrayed my trust, and I had honestly almost shot at them.

I didn't tell anyone where I was going. I just wanted a weekend backpacking trip around a lesser known state park to take my mind off things. When I put my backpack down to take a quick rest, I leaned back, thinking the railing would hold my weight.

It didn't, and I went tumbling down a hill, smacking into a few trees before groaning at the bottom.

I heard my femur and tibia snap under my other leg, my arm bent backwards in a way the joint shouldn't allow, and I practically felt my brain smash to the front of my skull, definitely concussed.

If I tried to drag myself up the hill, I passed out from the pain. My elbow was hyperextended, I probably wouldn't ever be able to move it properly again. The entire length of my leg felt shattered. I couldn't even let myself drift off; if I fell asleep with a concussion, I might not wake up.

My lips are cracked, but my water was inside my backpack on top of the hill. I even have service out here, I've heard my phone ring once or twice. Too bad it's up an easy but impossible climb.

I've been laying here for days. Nobody is coming to help, nobody even knows where I am. The nights out here aren't peaceful anymore, I've been hearing and seeing things that can't be real, the more I tell myself they're hallucinations, the more aggressive they become. I can't even shoot myself, my guns on top of the hill.

All I can do is wait for an animal to find me, or thirst to finish me off.

Wasps Are Assholes

Wasps are fucking assholes, stupid shitty sons of whores that fuck you up if you come too close.

Sorry, got a little mad there.

I made a little game out of it. If I saw one on the ground, I stomped it. If I caught one in a cup, I'd throw it in the microwave and zap it. If I caught one in a glue trap, I'd grab a snack and watch it slowly starve.

You may call be a sociopath, you're probably right, but again, fuck wasps.
Some species lay their eggs in living hosts, so that they can hatch inside the body and eat the host from the inside, keeping them alive as long as possible.

I can't imagine a worse death, anything that starts life out like that HAS to be a trash animal, right?

I noticed a nest forming outside my patio. Fuck. I got some gas and knocked them out, then brought them inside for the fun to begin. I got a look from a neighbor wearing a weird hoodie, but shrugged it off.

Wasp venom is actually capable of paralyzing some prey. I'm not sure how much it would take to stunt a person, but I think they'd go into shock first. Little assholes can't even fight a proper duel, they just make their prey weak and then torment them.

I came home from work after buying a lighter and some twine, I had planned a "witch pyre" death, for some of the remaining wasps from the nest. I put the container I kept them in inside the refrigerator, to make them fall asleep first, before I felt a sharp pain in my neck.

Shit! One of them must have gotten out. I reached up to slap my neck but my arm didn't move. My legs gave out and I crashed to the floor.

I could only stare in a daze at my neighbor, only he didn't look like himself. His eyes were compound, and his mouth had pincers coming out of it.

I woke up on my bed later, tied down to my bed. An IV was stuck in my arm, and my neighbor stood up, as if he'd been waiting.

"You made them hurt." The words came out in a weird click, but I understood them somehow. "They cried out for me for so long. I am finally here." Wasps crawled out of his arms and legs, jabbing their stingers into me.

"My children. Bhramari loves you all." He grinned. I whimpered as I felt hundreds of little needles jab into me.

I woke up in a daze to an empty apartment, still tied down, IV still inserted. I tried to move, but the straps were tight and I was weak from the stings. My body felt itchy all over, and I wanted to scratch so badly.

Then I noticed a bump moving in my arm, under the skin.

They hadn't just stung me.

They had laid their eggs in me.

The Drowned Kingdom

125,000 years ago, there was a city. It was not called Atlantis at the time, but history remembers it as such, so I shall call it by that name. The original name is impossible to pronounce in English, anyway.

This city was ruled by God. Or a powerful being calling itself God.

It matters not if this is the God that created the universe, or just an incredibly powerful magi. All that matters is he ruled over Atlantis, cultivating different forms of life and sending them outside the city to the rest of Earth.

We were his first. We were called the Nephilim. We are not giants, as depicted in that book you all use, but we look like the average human, only a little taller, and covered in brown fur.

We lived among him, not as equals, but as peers. He created humans in our image, starting with a man and a woman, and sent them off into Earth on their own.

He gave us the option to leave, but we declined. We enjoyed Atlantis, living with our God king, learning the secrets of the universe in a never ending library of knowledge.

He left us, for a while. He claimed he needed to travel to distant planets, to see how other creations and creators were doing, to see how his version of life compared to others.

He came back 5000 years after he left, frowning the whole time. He did not tell us what he had seen, but he had decided to start his world over. He claimed the humans were flawed, as well as the Nephilim, and most of the other creatures he had made.

In his absence, we had become self-sufficient. We learned the magic behind the machines that ran Atlantis, and often helped the humans in their times of need. We had grown fond of them, as our brothers and sisters on this Earth. So, five of us made a pact in blood, using the old Magic. All we had to do was find the courage to go through with it.

God spent weeks planning the end. Finally it began to rain, flooding the Earth and killing thousands. The only reason it stopped, and the only reason life continues on Earth, is we chained God to Atlantis, and sank it to the bottom of the seas.

You may search for it, if you wish. You won't find it, it is too far down for any humans to reach, with or without your vehicles, but I will not forbid you from searching if you desire.

The pact had a drawback, of course. Five of us agreed, and now only one of us remains.

In order to chain God to the sunken city, one of us had to hold him back. This was both simple and impossible, as it only required one of us to stay in the city with him.

During this time, God could do anything, except leave the city. We spent eons underwater in the dark, with an omnipotent monster bent on destroying the planet. The entire time we would be down there, we would feel the sensation of drowning, without the relief of death. In addition, God could torment us, both with physical pain, and mental anguish, until our very souls deteriorated, and fell apart.

When this happened, the next one of us would swim down to the city, and take their place, suffering in the dark waters for as long as they could hold out. The order had been decided in the pact, and the pact had been sealed in blood.

In the meantime, the four of us lived around the humans, only getting involved if we had to. In more recent times, your kind had invented better technology, so we had to hide more often, although we were sometimes potted nonetheless. There are legends about us, we even made ourselves a nickname and introduced ourselves as such.

You call us Bigfoot, but we are the Nephilim. We have endured more pain than any other living thing, in order to protect life on this planet.

Which leads me to my dilemma. I am the last of the Nephilim, I can feel my sister fading away, her skin torn, her soul shattered, her lungs demanding breath that would never come. There is not much of her left, and I know that I must go down soon, as we promised years ago.

But the problem is, I feel God was right. There is something fundamentally WRONG with the humans, and while I was unsure for a long while, the events of this past century have convinced me.

I do not believe humans are worth saving.

I have seen your kind kill each other over belief and race. I have seen your kind refuse to protect your weaker members. I have seen your kind rob, steal, kill and rape throughout history, but this decade, it seems humans have lost the ability to care about each other.

I dream every night of the pain that would be inflicted on me, the hot metal hooks in my limbs, the water flooding into my body, the darkness all around me.

I cannot consider it worth it.

He may come for me when he gets out, but at least it will be over quick. The alternative is to suffer for beings that would not even consider doing the same, even for members of their own species.

I do not know how much longer she will last. I feel her in my head, begging for death, screaming for relief, waiting for me to take the mantle as martyr. I wonder how it feels, her living with the knowledge that when she gives up, all life will end.

I have freed myself of this burden. I await the end.

It will start soon, within the decade for sure.

This is your warning.

We gave you a chance, and you have failed.

Story Time

Everyone has a story they HAVE to tell. Sometimes it's their life story, sometimes it's the events of a traumatic childhood, assault, or something amazing happening, like how they met their wife or husband.

Have you ever had that feeling where the story you HAVE to tell has absolutely nothing to do with you?

I have, all the time. I think that's why so many people try to be authors, it helps them say what they have to say, without having to be vocal. It's why I like writing, it lets me tell a story without having to live it. It's why I tried so hard to create, to edit, to publish.

But sometimes, our stories aren't meant to be. Life takes over, we lose our creative spark, or the motivation to go back and revise previous notes. Sometimes it just doesn't happen.

I went for a midnight walk alone to clear my head. This was a stupid idea, people across the city had been vanishing, but in that moment I just wanted to exist outside, both mentally and physically.

The abridged version is that I don't go to the gym as often as I should have, and the man abducted me very easily.

When I woke up, I was chained to a cellar wall. A giant man walked down the cellar stairs, just by looking at him I could tell he didn't skip his gym days like I did. No wonder it was so easy to get here.

Without a word, the massive man sat next to me, looking right at me. "Tell me a story," he asked.

"What? Get me out of here!" I yelled, starting to panic as my situation set in. The man shrugged, then suddenly slammed down, pinning my left arm to the ground. I had no chance of lifting this man, and had trouble breathing under his weight as he peeled the skin off my pinky finger, finally grinning at me before craving the base and yanking it off with a sickening rip. "Tomorrow then," he declared, dropping a pack near me and leaving.

After I was done crying, I opened the pack. Inside was a water bottle, energy bars, a notebook, pens, and a flashlight.

I've been working ever since. Writing down as many ideas as I can, working them out and through like never before. If the story is too short, too long, or doesn't make sense, the man wordlessly pins me down, having his fun with a different finger.

It got progressively harder to write, my stumps ached every time I grasped a pen. The floor is covered with more blood than I know I've lost, so I think I've also found where those other people wound up.

When I wrote a story about one of the missing people, he sliced the skin off my entire right hand, before yanking it off like he did my fingers.

I'm fucked. I'm so worried for tomorrow.

I was right handed.

My Son Shouldn't Exist

I opened an Einstein–Rosen bridge (the wormhole, for the dumbest of you) using an impossible combination of exotic matter, high pressure, and a collection of quarks with negative mass.

As soon as it opened, I leapt through, forgetting I might be spaghettified or trapped in an endless void for the rest of my life.

I ended up in a parallel world. It was still Earth, just with significant or subtle historical changes, depending on the situation.

In this world, China no longer existed, the American empire covered more territory north, presidents and world leaders were different, but with similar policies.

I met my girlfriend a few days inside this world. I wanted to explore as much as I could, and that included getting to know people. I didn't plan on falling in love, but I did. We moved in together after six months, I prepared a book explaining wormholes and my work. The pregnancy wasn't planned either, but was still a pleasant surprise. We decided not to get married right away, we already felt more together then most married couples.

Good things never last, though.

My son was born on a Tuesday night, and as soon as he took his first breath, I knew something was wrong. He never cried, nor did he seem to soil himself. I'd go to change him after noticing a smell and he'd be perfectly clean. We got a puppy, but the little thing wouldn't go near him, just shivering in the corner.

When he turned five, my son destroyed this world.

At least, I think just this world. It's entirely possible he destroyed my own, also. Maybe all possible worlds. I don't think it matters.

The only people left in existence are my girlfriend and I. Our son is a good boy, he loves us, but doesn't understand his power. Fuck, I don't understand it either, but it probably stems from his parents originating from two different worlds.

He's a reality bender, he can change the world around him to suit his needs. When you're five years old, your life is your parents, and so that became his focus, getting rid of everything else, literally. We were devastated, but put on a brave face. We tried to get him to bring the world back, but he said he didn't know how.

We have fun, I'll admit. He'll conjure a zoo, a forest with camping gear, an empty arcade where the games are free. He tries to make us happy, and sometimes he even succeeds.

Today he created a beach, nice and warm, with cold wine in a cooler for me and my girl. In my old life, this would be paradise. My girlfriend slams half the bottle down, tears trickling down her face. I wrap my arms around her as we watch our son swim into the waves, and whisper to her that everything will be alright when he's older.

Oh, but that feels like a lie.

Ledges

I saw a man standing on the side of a bridge, so I ran to help him.

I was doing what everybody should, helping someone who was in trouble. I talked to him slowly, letting him calm himself down.

His name was Nick. He wasn't very attractive, but he certainly wasn't as ugly as he insisted.

"I'm tired of seeing all these people around me with a purpose." He explained. "Everyone's running around, getting married, advancing in careers, raising kids, and I'm just...alone. Closed off. It's my own fault, I've always been like that, and I just assumed something would change…" He trailed off, so I squeezed his hand. "I thought I'd do more with my life besides wait for it to be over."

I nodded. I told him I knew that feeling, of wandering through life with no purpose or goals. Not feeling like you belong anywhere you go. Never feeling like you were understood by anyone around you.

"What if I die without anybody having ever truly understood me?" Nick asked, his tone revealing this may be his worst fear.

I told him I didn't know; I didn't understand him either, but I was starting to. I told him such, even explaining how I was a random stranger and my advice shouldn't be taken as gospel. He seemed to appreciate my honesty, even when I was blunt; I told him life had more bad days than good, it was up to us to find our own purpose, our own reason for waking up every morning, especially when all the reasons other people have hold no excitement or place for people like us.

He smiled, showing me that everything was going to be okay with him from then on. He looked lighter, full of hope, ready for whatever the world could throw at him. "Thank you. For caring. For stopping to talk to me. Most people would've just kept walking, or called the police." I grabbed him in a tight hug as he began to sob. He was a short guy, but a little heavy, it took a lot for me to wrap my arms around his whole chest.

I felt his tears hit my shoulder, before I pushed him backwards off the bridge, and into the dark water below.

What? It's no fun if they already WANT to die.

Constipation Isn't Funny, Guys.

I don't know how to explain this to the authorities, or the doctors, or anyone, really, so I'm writing this here in the hopes that someone can help me stop what I've started.

It started a week ago, on my birthday. I had turned twenty five, and had gone to a Japanese restaurant with some friends to celebrate. When I went to the bathroom, my friend thought it would be funny if she ordered me something gross on the menu, and ordered me an undercooked squid egg.

Being the adventurous guy I am, and wanting to impress the ladies, I ate it.

It was disgusting. Would not recommend it.

The rest of our meal was great, we had rice, hibachi, and sake. After dinner, we split the bill, and went our separate ways.

The next day I drank my pot of coffee, and prepared for my morning routine. Shit. Shave. Shower.

Only I didn't have to go, despite the coffee.

Weird, but not abnormally so. I didn't think much of it, and went on with my day.

Three days later I had to call in because the pressure in my gut was so bad. I went to the store and got laxatives, drank more coffee than anyone should, ordered Taco Bell for lunch and dinner, but still, nothing would pass.

I spent both my days and nights researching constipation. It was always funny when it happened to other people, or in the context of jokes, but like diarrhea, it wasn't so funny when you were the victim.

The more time passed, the more I read, and the more I read, the more scared I became. I didn't want my intestines to burst from blockage, or excess bile to be reabsorbed into my body, poisoning me. I decided on day six that if I didn't have a bowel movement by the next day, I would go to the emergency room.

After eating breakfast the next morning. I felt it. I had never been so excited to take a dump before in my life. I practically skipped to the bathroom, as fast as my bloated body would allow. I sat down on the toilet, pulled out my phone, and prepared myself.

I gave anal birth to what felt like an elephant cub. I actually screamed, grasping the shower curtain for leverage. It all poured out at once, one giant, disgusting blockage of feces. I thought I'd have to start taking painkillers afterwards. Imagine the biggest dump you've ever taken, and multiply that by a week's worth of waste.

I lay shivering on the ground. I might need to start therapy after this. I almost wished I had weighed myself, for a before and after comparison. That made me chuckle, then burst into laughter; this was such a gross, ridiculous situation! Tears rolled down my eyes, from both ass pain and hysterical laughter.

As soon as I started laughing, a large, pink tentacle shot out from my toilet bowl. My laughter turned to a scream as it slapped my leg, then tried to grasp onto me.

I darted away, and screamed again when I looked inside my toilet.

There was a massive amount of poop, and swimming inside it was a bright, pink, squid like creature. It looked larger than anything that would've come out a person, and it actually hissed at me, rolling it's weird eyes up to see its parent.

I panicked, and did the first thing I could think of. I flushed the toilet. The squid-thing resisted, so I grabbed my plunger and forced it down, until the vacuum of the drain pulled it down and out of sight.

I woke up on the bathroom rug, the smell of feces and blood permeating in the small room. I don't know when I passed out, but it was nighttime when I woke up.

I tried to think of a rational explanation, but came up short. I had to assume I just had poop madness, that the backed up bile had caused me to hallucinate, or that the pain had just made me that woozy where I needed to imagine something going on.

I made a massive turd, possibly a world record, to the point where my mind needed to make something out of it to cope. I tried to stand up, and felt a shuddering pain in my butt. The poop was so large, that I definitely needed to go see a doctor as soon as possible.

I waddled over to the car, setting paper towels in my pants to avoid soaking my underwear in blood. During the drive, I noticed a large number of police cars and ambulances out. It had snowed two days ago, so I assume the people leaving quarantine had forgotten how to drive when it's winter.

The drive itself wasn't long, but I spent it grunting and thinking of an explanation for what happened. No doctor was going to look at my butt and assume there wasn't some weird, sexual kink gone wrong. We've all heard the "I fell on it by accident" jokes that doctors tell, and I just hoped that the truth would convince them.

I had been constipated for a week, took a giant dump, and might need stitches. Embarrassing, but not impossible.

My mind kept drawing back to that squid thing. Maybe it was the gross egg I ate, my unconscious mind just brought it forward when I finally had a movement? I decided I'd tell the doctor I saw some hallucinations after, but wouldn't go into specifics.

I got a mask from the front desk, told registration I had a rectal injury, and waddled over to a seat to wait.

There was a huge list of patients ahead of me. Most people in our community were part of the "I don't need to wear a mask, don't tell me what to do," subgroup, so I assumed karma had caught up with them and they needed to get tested.

I pulled out my phone to speed up the wait. I had a few missed texts and calls, some dating two days ago. Jesus, was I really unconscious for two whole days? After taking a shit? I made a mental note not to ever mention this story to anyone.

An old man was trying to get my attention. I looked up from my phone. He pointed at the television, on a new station, and pointed at the table next to me, where the remote was held, then pointed up.

I used my genius level intellect to translate. He wanted me to turn the volume up. I obliged, even turning subtitles on in case he was hard of hearing. He gestured back by making a heart with his hands, and I grinned under my mask.

"Authorities are calling it 'The Toilet Creature.' They aren't sure about its origins, and pictures taken by victims indicate it is a medium sized, pink squid."

Wait what? I cranked the volume up higher. Pictures of a squid inside a toilet bowl flashed on the screen.

"Animal control is unsure where the attacks started, but it appears to be using the sewer systems as its home." The reporter went on. "There have been as many as twenty injuries today, and two child fatalities. Police are urging anyone with any information to come forward."

I leaned back in my chair, ignoring the dull throb of my anus.

I could go to the police, but what would I even say? "Hey, my name is Dan, I shit a squid out two days ago, hope that helps, bye!"

No. They'd never believe me, and even if they did, it wouldn't help them much.

What do I do here? I'm sitting in the waiting room, more and more people are filing in, and I'm low on the list to see a doctor.

Scenery along the Route

The princess and the wizard sat upon the edge of a cliff, watching the world vanish.

"I don't get it," she mumbled. "You slayed the dragon, I saved the kingdom. Shouldn't we get a 'happily ever after'?"

He lit his pipe, inhaling sweet tobacco. "Normally, yes. But it appears our narrative is ending."

"Narrative?" The princess quizzically asked.

He blew a circle of smoke out. "There are three types of people. There are Writers, Readers, and Livers. It is the Liver's job to live their lives, the Writer's job to document the Livers life, and the Readers job to observe the Livers life." He leaned back, watching the mountains around them twinkle out of existence.

"But what does that MEAN?" She asked. "Why is our world disappearing?"

"Because we have finished living our story." He answered calmly.

"But we didn't die! I can go home, and marry the prince, the nightmare is over!"

The wizard chuckled. "No, sweetheart. If you were a Reader, maybe, but we were born Livers. We only exist to be recorded and observed."

"Observed by who?"

"Those above us," he gestured to the sky. "A Writer is writing this, and soon some Readers will read it. Once they're done, we won't have any more reason to exist, so…" He made a 'pfft' sound, pushing his hands apart.

"What about the rest of our lives? Why don't we get to live them?"

"They aren't important to this Narrative anymore."

She scoffed. "That's not fair! You're saying some people only exist to fulfill their story, then they disappear? Who would make a world like that?"

He gave her a mournful look. "I'm sure they don't mean to. See that forest over there, disappearing? It's as real as anything, but to someone watching us from above, it's nothing more than words on a page. Just like you and me."

"But other stories have happy endings."

"If their narrative explains a person's happy ending, then they get to live it. It appears our Writer had a limited amount of space to explain our world, so we have to stop existing once they run out of room."

"Are they God?" She asked in a soft voice.

"In a way," he answered. "But there's an Author above them also, and one above that, and so on. Just like there are stories below us, we ourselves act as Readers when we tell them."

"What's at the top?" She asked, the cliffs around them beginning to dissipate.

He shrugged, arms starting to flicker in and out of existence. "We're getting to the end, apparently there's no more story to tell. We saved the kingdom."

"Why did it matter?" She asked quickly, before the wizard could disappear.

"Did you enjoy the adventure?"

She paused. "I- Yes."

"That's it, then" he grinned. "It's all about the scenery along the route." He said, before he vanished completely.

She sat alone, watching her world slip away all around her.

"But I don't want to go," she said, before she faded away.

About the Author

Matt Gall is some weird guy who lives in Wisconsin. He enjoys reading, camping, writing (duh), and hiking. Matt lives alone with his cat Walter, whose company he prefers to most of the general population. He will always accept any drink with whiskey in it, so feel free to offer him one if you ever see him (hey, it's worth a shot).

Made in the USA
Monee, IL
11 April 2021